# RESCUE

AT

# LAKE WILD

# RESCUE AT LAKE WILD

### TERRY LYNN JOHNSON

**HOUGHTON MIFFLIN HARCOURT**
BOSTON   NEW YORK

hmhbooks.com

The text was set in Carre Noir Std

Jacket illustration by Maike Plenzke

Map art by Maike Plenzke

Cover design by Kaitlin Yang

Interior design by Kaitlin Yang

*The Library of Congress Cataloging-in-Publication data is available.*

ISBN: 978-0-358-33485-9

Manufactured in the United States of America
DOC 10 9 8 7 6 5 4 3 2 1
4500820218

*In memory of Aunt Mae,*
*who somehow always knew about the fishing incidents,*
*and usually blamed them on John.*

JACK'S

*Little Hawk Lake*

trail

BEAVER
LODGE

MR. KANG'S

*Lake Wild*

MADI'S

MARSH

HAWK LAKE ROAD

*The least I can do is speak out for those who cannot speak for themselves.*

—Jane Goodall

# 1

I HEAR IT AGAIN.

Urgent chattering reaches us from the mound of sticks and mud just off the bow of our boat.

"We're going to have to do it," I say, and then can't help add, "I told you they were here."

As an animal whisperer, I know these things, but sometimes I have to remind certain people.

A breeze catches the boat and swings us around the anchor line. The channel's empty except for the beaver lodge, the three of us, and one bored dog.

"We're sure the parents aren't coming back, Madi?" Aaron asks.

"You saw their parents," I say. "They're not coming." We've been here almost two hours to make sure there were no other adults in the lodge.

Finally Jack says, "Let's do it already."

"Before you say I should do it because I'm smallest," Aaron says, "let me remind you I've been the rescuer the last two times."

He's talking about when we boosted him into a tree to save a raccoon that turned out not to need saving. Okay, I was wrong that one time. But the day we lowered him from the window by his feet to save the baby bird? That bird would have died without us.

"Out of the three of us, you're the easiest to hang by the feet," I say reasonably.

"It's not my turn." Aaron shifts on the aluminum seat. "And I'm not that small."

"We've never done *this* before," Jack says. "So it starts over."

"What starts over?"

"Turns," Jack says.

Adjusting the tiller handle, I move to sit next to Aaron in the middle of the boat. "We should play for it." I hold up a fist, the universal sign for rock-paper-scissors. "So it's fair."

The three of us stick our fists together. Jack's black

Lab, Lid, pokes his nose into the circle too, ever hopeful that we're about to unveil food.

"One, two, *three!*"

"No!" Aaron yells at our scissors to his paper. "Rigged!"

"I'd take your shirt off if I were you," Jack advises. "So it doesn't get stuck and snag you down there. We probably wouldn't be able to pull you up."

Aaron pales but tries to look brave. "I always end up doing it," he grumbles, reaching behind his back to pull off his T-shirt. The hot July sun bounces off his blinding white torso.

Aaron scowls at us and then glances over the side of the boat. He studies the brown water and mutters something about leeches.

"Maybe you should keep your shirt on for protection," I suggest, eyeing his stick-thin arms covered in rust-brown freckles, and his pale shoulder blades that could cut a breakfast sausage.

"Are they even still alive?" Aaron says. "I can't hear them anymore."

*He's right.* There'd been no sounds from the

lodge in the last few minutes we've been sitting here arguing.

Earlier, we'd found two adult beavers floating dead on the other side of the channel. Jack, as usual, had wanted to investigate the crime scene immediately. But the noises from the lodge mean babies inside. Those babies will starve to death if we don't rescue them.

We've been waiting here long enough to know there are no other adult beavers coming to take care of them. But how long have the young ones been alone in there? Maybe they're starved already.

"Shhh!" I say. "Listen."

We still our movements in the boat and drift. An enthusiastic frog trills next to us. The wind rustles the leaves of trembling aspen towering above. The water gently laps at the aluminum beneath us. We strain to hear anything. The silence stretches.

A long, high-pitched noise erupts from Lid's rear end. It echoes strangely from the bottom of the boat, sounding like an optimistic elephant. Surprised, Lid looks behind him.

Aaron and Jack both burst out laughing. It's so hard to keep boys focused.

"Guys, I don't hear them. Maybe we waited too long." Maybe the little beavers are just too weak now to make noise and desperately need help right this very second. I grab the anchor and haul it up. "We have to hurry!"

I yank at the oars and thrust the boat up onto the muddy bank of the lodge. Lid jumps out first, followed by Jack, who ties us off on a log. Aaron warms up, swinging his arms, further accentuating his shoulder blades.

Stepping onto the latticed sticks, I peer at a section of the lodge's roof that's been ripped apart, most likely by wolves. But the predators haven't gotten through. The only way into an indestructible beaver lodge is underwater.

"Okay. You're looking for the opening to the tunnel," I say to Aaron. "It'll be hidden among all the sticks. Hopefully it'll be wide enough for you to fit. You can breathe once you get into the chamber. It'll be a room above water like a den. That's where you'll find the baby beavers."

Aaron nods while staring at the lodge. He examines the murky water.

I watch him uneasily and think about when we'd

boosted him into that tree. He'd spent most of the time clutching the trunk and yelling for us to bring him down. And when we'd lowered him for the bird he insisted over and over, "Pull me up!"

*This* is actually dangerous. If Aaron panics, he could drown for real. He could get lost under there, or get caught on something, like Jack said.

A fluttery feeling builds inside my chest. Did Jane Goodall let someone else face aggressive chimps at the Tanzania research center? No.

It should be me.

I glance at my bare legs under my Nike shorts. My arms are exposed too. At least my hair is out of the way, woven into two braids.

I had told Aaron what to look for as if I was sure what I was doing. As if I'd broken into plenty of beaver lodges. Even after all my field time spent observing beavers in the wild, I've never seen what a lodge looks like inside.

Images flash of getting trapped underwater, of being lost in the maze of sticks, of not finding the tunnel. What if I make it into the chamber but it's not like what I'd read? What if it's full of water and I can't breathe?

I steel myself. The beavers need help or they're going to die. Someone has to get them. It'll be okay. "Wait for me here," I say, stepping toward the edge of the water.

And then I jump in.

# 2

## THE WATER'S THE COLOR OF TEA.

That's my first problem once I open my eyes. I can't see a thing.

I kick up to the surface to get my bearings and take a huge gulp of air. When I dive back down, my last sight is the worried expressions on my friends' faces.

Slowly, I feel my way along the edge of the lodge, pulling myself down. The sticks are naked and slippery. I try to scan around me but see only particles of mud and weird things floating in the pale light from the surface.

The light disappears the farther down I go. I crash into a root or something and cut the back of my hand. Continuing by feel, I grope the maze of sticks, wishing hard that I knew for sure where the opening would be.

*It's going to be here.* It has to be. That's how beavers make homes. They build this big castle of sticks and hide their door somewhere so that no other animals can get in.

I'm pretty sure I know how to get into a beaver lodge. But I didn't expect it to be quite so . . . dark.

The idea of leeches didn't sound that bad when I was sitting in the boat. Now, I feel things brushing against me. I slap madly at a leaf sticking to my left thigh. My heart pounds. I'm going to need to breathe soon.

*Calm down.*

Just as I'm about to go up for another gulp of air, I feel an opening chewed into the wall of logs. I pull myself into the center—it's narrow and stabby. The skin on my shoulders scrapes raw as if I'm being attacked by a giant metal rake.

I pull myself faster. My lungs are near bursting. *How much farther?*

Is this even the right tunnel?

Am I going to die down here?

My shoulders wedge. And then my head pops out of the water. My own gasping sounds loud in my ears. It echoes off the walls of . . . wherever I've come up.

Inside all those branches and sticks is blackness.

The air feels muggy damp. But the biggest thing I notice is the smell. It's fetid and musky like my nana's root cellar. I imagine it's how a bathroom packed with wet weasels would smell.

I look around. The dark is so thick, it seems to have a shape hovering over me. *Do not be afraid of the dark.*

After I gulp more air, I still so I can listen.

"Anyone in here?"

I wait. The murmurs and noises we've been hearing for the past hour are gone. The beavers have shut right up.

Maybe we *are* too late. Have I come all this way for nothing? Have the babies slowly died in here alone, waiting for someone to come save them? Wondering where their parents were?

There!

A rustling on my right. It sounds like something moving slowly away. Blindly, I reach out, groping. I feel a hump of mud, stones, sticks, and then . . . fur.

"Ah, ha! There you are." *I knew it!*

I pluck up the baby beaver and bring it close to my chest. It's surprisingly dry, with a slick coat of fur. It sits quietly in my hand and feels about as heavy as one of my dad's shoes.

From my field time, I know beavers usually have more than one baby, or kit. I reach out again and encounter another furry body about the same size. Then I continue my search until I'm satisfied there aren't any more.

Juggling the bodies to my chest, I consider my next problem. Now that I've found them, how am I going to carry them out?

Gently, I stuff the two kits inside my tank top. Their fur tickles the bare skin of my belly. I tuck the bottom of my tank into my shorts, cradling the bulges carefully with one hand. Surely beavers know how to hold their breath?

I take my own huge breath, flip around, and dive back into the water.

It's much easier coming out now that I know where I'm going. More sunlight penetrates the closer I get. When I break the surface, my friends, standing on the bank of mud, cheer.

"Were they dead?" Jack asks at the same time that Aaron says, "We thought you were dead!"

Lid cocks his eyebrows at me.

I flop at their feet, inching out of the water on my side like a seal coming ashore. And then I peel up the bottom of my tank.

Two brown beaver kits sit on my stomach and blink. I've never felt more proud of a rescue in my life. I stare back at them with awe and profound relief.

Aaron points at me in horror. "Leeches!"

# 3

A GIANT LEECH STICKS TO THE BACK OF my knee, sucking my blood like a fat, glossy vampire.

I can handle that. But the millions of tiny, wiggly leeches all over my legs? That's a different story.

I sit up. "Get them off!"

"I'm not touching a swarm of leeches!" Aaron yells back.

Jack pokes at the leeches with a stick, fascinated. I knock his stick aside and brush madly down my thighs and shins while trying to hold still for the kits crouching in my lap. They look horrified for me.

To my relief, the small leeches swipe off easily. They're like black exclamation marks falling off me. But the big daddy isn't going to give up. It's longer than a finger, flat, wide, and determined.

"Just rip it out before it sucks you dry," Jack says.

I nudge at the leech. "It's stuck on both ends!"

"Cool," Jack says. "It's sucking from its mouth *and* its butt!"

"It's got two mouths," Aaron says. He knows a lot about weird things like this. "You have to break the seal."

I can't see it well since it's behind my knee. I point my foot in the air. "One of you has to do it."

With all the commotion, the kits start up an alarmed *mewing* and hug each other with their little arms. I cradle them protectively with one hand while reaching behind my knee with the other. One end of the leech comes off when I scratch at it. It stands up and waves around like a tiny person looking for a fight. The hole it leaves in my skin starts bleeding.

"Gross!" Jack says. He grins, grabs the leech, and yanks.

"*Yeow!*"

That gets the leech off me, but now it's stuck to Jack. His grin disappears. He flicks his hand around before using his stick to dislodge it. Sadly, he's not bleeding like me.

"You're gushing all over the place," Aaron points

out. Blood runs down my wet leg and turns the heel of my Keen sandal a watery pink.

"That's not the biggest problem," I say.

We all look at the kits huddled on my lap.

Everyone knows I'm not allowed to bring home animals anymore. *Not one more stray* or I'll never get to meet Jane Goodall in Stratton. The Jane Goodall Institute is putting on a gala. Dad got us tickets. And the best part—backstage passes. It's just Dad and me going, and we get to stay in a hotel with a fountain in the lobby.

I *need* to meet Jane Goodall. Not only is my room plastered with Jane Goodall posters and stories, and I've seen every single documentary about her life's work, and I've gone as Jane Goodall for Halloween every year since I was seven, but I have vital things to ask.

I want to know about her observations in the wild for important discoveries. I want to show her my notes from my own observations. Mostly, I want to know how she did it. Not many people would pack up and move to Tanzania all alone. She made sacrifices. I want to ask how she knew what to do. How did she *know* in her heart she was meant to save animals?

I also have to tell her about my nana, who was a wildlife rehabilitator. Since I was Nana's apprentice, it's up to me to brag about her.

Mom says I must not understand what Nana did if I want to do it when I grow up. It's too much work. She thinks I was too young when Nana died to remember how hard it was to try to rehabilitate orphaned and injured wildlife so they can be released back in the wild.

But I did understand. I do remember. I remember Nana showing me how to safely hold baby birds so I didn't crush them. And the feeling I had when it came time to release them. I remember the sharp, feral scent of the raptor enclosure. The way the chemical tang filled my nose when Nana sanitized the mammal crates.

I watched her syringe-feed orphaned, bald squirrels, and heal injured skunks and rabbits and groundhogs and even a porcupine. And I remember her telling me how to listen to them. How to know their emotions with my heart. Nana knew animals. She knew how to make them feel at ease when they needed it most. She called herself an animal whisperer.

In the four years since the cancer, I've continued what Nana taught me. There was the box of hairless mice, a turtle, a squirrel, two birds, a rabbit, and last week, a tomcat that was hungry.

Without Nana, though, I've been doing it in secret. You can't keep wildlife without a special license. But also Mom says it's dangerous and I'm too young to take on the responsibility. She doesn't seem to understand. Without Nana here, who will help the animals?

Nana told me I'm a natural, that I must take after her. That when it came to knowing how to handle animals, I have an instinct no one else in our family has. It's a calming presence that can't be taught, but that animals can sense.

Maybe *I* should've sensed that ungrateful tomcat was going to spray our porch with a nasty smell and be *the last straw,* as Mom put it.

Now if I bring any more animals home, I won't be allowed to go to Stratton to meet Jane Goodall. I'm already packed, with a multipage list of questions ready. It's two weeks away.

I ponder what to do as I run a finger over the head of the smallest kit. He's wet now after our swim. "This one is called Phragmites."

"You mean the weed?" Aaron asks.

I shrug. "I just like the word."

"Weird," Jack says under his breath.

Phrag clutches my finger in both his hands as if thanking me for rescuing him. Each of his fingers ends in a fat nail, which explains the pink scratches on my belly.

The kits' back feet have even longer nails, with dark webbing between their toes. They both have small round tails. The larger kit is a darker brown than Phrag. He's shaped like a rectangle.

"That one looks like a furry lunch cooler," Aaron says.

"Good name," I say.

Cooler also grabs my hand and noses it, perhaps looking for warmth. They're both shivering. I bring them closer to my neck and they nuzzle me.

"What are we going to do with them?" Aaron asks. "We can't take them to the clubhouse like usual."

Aaron has a point. After that tomcat, Mom will be suspicious of what I do now. Where can I keep them? I just wanted to rescue the kits—I didn't think everything through.

"I have an idea." I set them down so I can climb

into the boat. Grabbing my backpack, I dig out my cell phone, push a button, and then put it on speaker.

"Willow Grove Veterinary Clinic," answers a crisp voice.

"You have the vet on speed dial?" Jack says.

I motion for him to shut up. "Hi. I'm calling to ask if you take in beaver kits that've been tragically orphaned."

"Beavers? Well, no, we can't do that. How old are they?"

"Oh, I'm just asking a hypothetical question. I don't actually have any. But if someone *had* rescued a beaver kit, about the size . . . of a squash, how old do you think it would be?"

"Hard to say. They're usually born in the spring, but not always. I don't know much about beavers. Except that they require a lot of time and socializing. Like a puppy. What've you gotten into this time, Madison?"

"What? No. No one here by that name. Anyway . . . gotta go." I hang up.

"Smooth," Aaron says. "You forgot about caller ID?"

"I panicked. No one can know we have them. What are we going to do with them?"

I don't know much about beavers either, besides

watching the loglike bodies of adults swim along the surface. It's a mystery what happens in a lodge. This is an excellent opportunity to learn more about them. Besides that, these guys need help.

"If you see something, do something," I whisper. My motto.

"We should take care of the kits," I say, stepping out of the boat. "We just need to find a place to keep them."

Jack perks up. "I can bring them home. There's lots of room and we've got the lake for them to swim. It's sort of perfect — having them there could help us solve the case, too."

Jack has wanted to be a game warden since he discovered *Game Warden TV*. He's always looking for poaching cases to solve, and he's even been training Lid, with our help, to be his detector dog.

Aaron makes a strangled noise, and points behind me.

I turn just in time to see Lid stuffing Phrag into his mouth.

# 4

*"NO!"*

All three of us lunge toward the dog. Lid immediately spits out his victim. I scoop up the little fur ball to check for damage. Phrag's covered in dog goober but seems unharmed. Lid has the decency to look sheepish when I glare at him.

"He wasn't going to hurt the kit," Jack says. "He was just trying to play."

Here's a story about Lid. When Jack and his family brought him home from the pound, the first thing the dog did was dive into the garbage can. They put a swinging cover on their can to keep him out. Lid got his name from being caught too many times wearing the plastic lid around his neck. That dog has an eating problem. Food, rotten food, socks, toy soldiers, earbuds, crayons, dirty diapers, and now beaver kits.

"Right," I say. "I guess that answers the question of whether we should take the kits to your house."

I turn to Aaron. He starts shaking his head. "No way. Uh-uh. We live in *town*. Where we going to keep two beavers?"

"They're small."

"My mom will kill me."

"Yeah, but it's not like *you* want to go to a gala. What can she do to you? Besides, you lost rock-paper-scissors. It's only fair. And you just have to keep them till I get back from Stratton."

I scoop up Cooler along with Phragmites and climb in the boat, shooting another dirty look at Lid. He gives me a confused expression as though he's forgotten about the time he tried to hork down a whole beaver kit.

"You want to go to your place and get the ATV?" Jack says, untying the bow line. His long black bangs fall into his eyes with a gust of wind.

I nod. It's the fastest way to get to Aaron's. "But it's in the garage. We'll have to go full stealth with the kits past the window if my parents are home."

I'm allowed to drive the all-terrain vehicle, or ATV, as long as we wear helmets, stay on our property, and don't go past third gear. Luckily our property stretches from Lake Wild all the way over to Birch Street and backs onto the ravine behind Aaron's.

First, we have to get home with the boat. I give the kits to Aaron for safekeeping while I start the motor. The beaver lodge sits in the center of a channel that flows from my lake, which is Lake Wild, to Jack's lake, which is Little Hawk. But Jack doesn't have an ATV or a clubhouse. I steer the boat to the right, and follow the channel into Lake Wild.

When we make it to my dock, I stuff Phragmites inside my shirt and Aaron hides Cooler.

"Clubhouse first," I whisper. I need supplies for the beavers.

We sprint across the backyard toward the shed that used to be for my mom's gardening things, but since she's been promoted at her legal firm, she's had no time for weeding. Besides being a good place to hold our meetings, it's also where I hide my animal rescues.

We swing open the door and pile in. I breathe a

sigh of relief and look around. My workbench along the back wall has my stash: eyedroppers, baby bottles, gloves, cotton balls, wood chips, water and feeding pans, some old stuffed bears of mine, cleaning supplies, and other tools of the trade I'd saved from Nana's. Two dog kennels stack in the corner along with some cardboard boxes, and there's a table with three chairs near the door.

I pull Phrag out to gently blow in his face so he'll get used to my smell, something I read in a rehabber magazine. I'm not sure if it's true or not. His dark, earnest eyes watch me back. He has a pleasant smell, not as musky as his lodge. Then I pick up one of the cardboard boxes and carefully place him inside. The beaver sits there looking a bit shell-shocked.

"Here." I wave to Aaron. "This'll be safer to carry them on the ATV."

When Cooler's lowered in, the kits cling to each other. Both of them immediately start up a wail. I hastily shut the lid, but the noise carries.

"It needs a blanket or something to protect them from bouncing," I say, "and to muffle the noise."

I have to risk going into the house. At least that way I'll see if anyone's home before we sneak past the window carrying a suspicious box.

Jack finds the clubhouse logbook and sits at the table, where Lid's already underneath checking for crumbs. "I'll start planning the investigation." Jack likes to make lists. Not surprisingly, he starts a column titled *Evidence.*

Aaron peers into the box and makes cooing noises. He complains a lot about my rescues, but I know he thinks it's fascinating.

I make my way to the side door of the house, hoping hard that my parents aren't around to ask questions. Mom can't suspect anything. Even though Dad grew up with a rehabber as his mom, he doesn't seem to know much about it. Only that he agrees with Mom about me not bringing home more strays.

The door opens soundlessly. I shuck off my wet sandals and tiptoe down the hall. I have to pass the kitchen, the place most likely to hold adults. I peek around the corner. No one there. *Nice.*

Scurrying past, I rummage in the hall closet until I

find a towel the same brown as the beavers. It looks old, so maybe no one will miss it.

I grab it along with a hot water bottle. And then throw them in the air when a voice behind me says, "Madi, you're bleeding all over the floor."

# 5

I SPIN AROUND TO FIND MY SISTER, MAR-ley, standing in the kitchen drinking out of the milk carton.

"You didn't use a glass," I say. "At least I can wipe up the blood. You can't wipe your germs off the carton."

Marley shrugs, replaces the milk, and closes the fridge with a hip.

"Where's the rest of your crew? What are you gremlins up to?" She points at me. "Why are you all wet and bleeding? And why do you have muck in your hair?"

I pat at my hair to discover it is indeed full of muck. Nice that no one bothered to mention it until now. "Will you drive us to Aaron's?"

"Of course not."

My sister is predictable, so my question works like

I'd planned. She sticks her earbuds back in and wanders away. At sixteen and a half, Marley is the perfect sitter. Since Mom and Dad are usually working, Marley's supposed to watch me. But as long as I stay out of her way, she leaves me alone. That works for both of us.

I start the kettle for the hot water bottle, something I use with baby animals. The first important thing is to keep them warm and dry. While I'm waiting for the water, I find a Band-Aid to stop my blood from making a trail through the house.

I'll use one of my old teddy bears to cover the hot water bottle. If you give orphans a pretend mother, they're less stressed. Nana told me this, so I know it's not just me presuming that orphans miss their moms.

One of the trickiest things about being an animal whisperer is to make sure you aren't imagining your own emotions onto the animal. I think of the beaver kits and wonder, will they really trust me, or do I just hope that?

My mind goes to the first few birds I'd tried to feed on my own. I didn't know enough to save them.

Some people might say they were just birds. That

birds don't have feelings or emotions. That they can't think like smarter animals such as monkeys. Not true! Birds are amazing. I read about scientists doing a study on crows, where the crows figured out how to drop rocks into a column of water to make the food in a connected tube rise. And then there are tailorbirds — they use the ropy stuff from plants to sew leaves together for a nest. I can't even sew patches onto my backpack.

The whole animal kingdom has fascinated me since the day Nana showed me a photo of chimpanzees with their lips stretched out, talking to Jane Goodall. The more I learn about each kind of animal, the more I want to help them.

I never imagined I'd one day be taking care of beaver kits, holding them in my hands, feeling how their fur is coarse and fuzzy. Seeing how they look at me with wet eyes and make noises like human babies.

After filling the bottle, I gather everything we'll need and head back to the clubhouse.

Once everyone's in the garage, Aaron climbs onto the ATV in his usual place on the queen seat at the back. I pass him the box of beavers to hold on his lap.

"Where am *I* going to sit now?" Jack says. The box takes up more space than I thought, and Jack's the biggest of the three of us.

"There's room behind me if you squish."

"How 'bout I drive and you squish?"

Aaron and I both make the same protesting snort, remembering the last time Jack drove. In answer I tighten my helmet and swing into the driver's seat. Jack grumbles but squeezes in behind me. Lid knows to follow along beside us.

"We'll take the trail then go up Birch Street," I say. It's the only way to get to Aaron's on the ATV. Otherwise we'd have to park the ATV on the trail, cross the ravine on foot, balance along the log, and then hike up the hill that leads to Aaron's backyard. I imagine crossing the log and accidentally dropping the box.

"We're not allowed to go on the road," Aaron reminds me.

"Only a few minutes. No one's going to see," I say. "We'll be quick and quiet."

But when we arrive at the road and then turn toward the bridge, I stop the ATV dead.

"Uh," Jack says.

The bridge and a section of the road are flooded out. But that isn't the worst part. There are people everywhere. Cars are parked along the shoulder with the Township maintenance truck. A police cruiser has its lights blinking red and blue. Men in coveralls and hip waders are holding poles, and police are setting up traffic cones to block the road. With the noise of the ATV engine, everyone stops what they're doing and turns to look at us.

"So not as quiet as I thought," I say.

"I told you not to go on the road!" Aaron sounds like a clucking hen when he's right.

One of the officers heads toward us.

"Go, go, go!" Jack screeches, prodding me in the back.

I whip us around, throwing up loose gravel, and take the first trail I see. It's lumpy and bushed in.

"Hurry!" Jack yells in my ear. "They're gonna catch us!"

The engine roars a complaint. We're going too fast for third gear. My toe itches to kick the shifter into fourth, but I'm in enough trouble with being on the road. And if I get caught with the box, how will I explain it?

I don't know where this trail goes. Luckily, I don't have time to worry about it while struggling to keep us from ditching. I wrestle the handlebars over some rocks. We bounce around a clump of striped maple. The large leaves cling to my face, momentarily blinding me. I swat them away, but then have to grab the handlebars again as we ride over a punky log lying across the trail.

"Are they following?" I yell over my shoulder. "Are we being chased?"

"We're all going to jail!" Aaron yells back.

The ATV dives down a steep embankment. I grip the brakes, making us skid out to the side like a sail filling with wind. I've just gained control again when we suddenly emerge into a giant swamp.

"Floor it!" Jack yells.

I speed up to get through, the mud spraying behind us. The engine begins to bog down, sounding like a dying cow. And then we lurch to a stop, stuck up to the axel.

# 6

**"RUN!"**

Jack dives off the ATV, falling into the mud. "Spread out. They won't be able to chase us alll!"

Aaron freezes, eyes wide, clutching the box.

When I slide off the ATV my feet sink to my shins. Each step makes sucking noises and smells like something Lid would eat. I take the box from Aaron. "Are they still following us?"

Aaron and I both listen, but there's no sound of pursuit. All I hear is Jack crashing through the bushes, followed by his delighted dog.

Aaron perches on the back of the ATV and lines himself up to jump. He leaps for solid ground but falls short, landing on his knees with a dull splat. His arms sink past his elbows.

"Maybe they gave up the chase." He eyes his muddy hands with distaste. "Do you have a winch?"

"No idea." I wade around the tires to get a better look at how stuck we are. Very.

Resting the box on the seat, I open the top and peek in. The kits are huddled and listless, mewing softly instead of bawling like they'd been doing. As if they didn't even have the strength to cry.

A sharp panic spears me. What am I doing running around with helpless animals? Have I learned nothing from my early, failed attempts at rescues? The kits need to be kept secure and quiet, not bouncing around in a box. What kind of animal whisperer forgets that?

I look around at our situation, thinking frantically. With Birch Street washed out, we're not going to make it to Aaron's. But *someone* needs to take care of the kits.

"Don't worry, guys." I close the lid and place the box on dry ground. "I'm going to bring you home now."

I'll have to hide them in the clubhouse like all the other animals I've saved. Maybe I'll get lucky and no one will notice. But first, we have to get out of here.

Aaron has given up trying to stay out of the mud.

He studies the front grill of the ATV, flips a lever, and pulls out a metal hook attached to a cable.

"How . . . you knew that was there this whole time?" I ask.

Aaron ignores me. The cable unrolls as he schlucks his way to a tree. He wraps it around the trunk. "There should be a button to pull in the cable," he says, pointing.

"How do you know this?" I push it and the winch tightens. I'm used to Aaron knowing things—he belongs to the Junior Engineers club at school—but he doesn't even own an ATV.

"It's just logical," Aaron says. "And physics. Keep pushing it."

Slowly, the winch motor pulls the ATV about a foot and a half ahead, which is enough to get us unstuck.

Aaron retrieves the cable and then climbs on the ATV. "I'll reverse it. You push in case we get stuck again."

"I'd rather do the reversing," I say, but he's already revving the gas.

The tires grab clumps of mud in their knobby tread. As I push, the mud flings out, slapping me in a cold, wet line up the front of my tank. It smells like loon poop.

But the ATV makes it to solid ground. We're back in business.

"Yay!" We bump fists.

That's when Jack decides it's safe to come out of hiding.

He takes a moment to look at me. "You've got a little something right here," he says with a grin, indicating his entire torso and face.

I flick a glob of mud at him.

# 7

AT THE CLUBHOUSE, I CAN TELL RIGHT
away that my troubles with the beaver kits have just
begun.

"You should give them milk," Jack says. "All babies
like milk. I don't blame him for not wanting that fake
stuff from a pail."

"Cow's milk is very bad for baby wildlife," I explain,
trying not to roll my eyes. I learned this basic rehabber
rule from Nana when I was six.

I struggle to get Cooler to accept the bottle. It con-
tains the usual formula: one part powder and two parts
water. I'd been lucky to find the right kind for beavers from the various formulas that I'd salvaged from
Nana's. Different animals have different needs for what

food they should eat. But even though this is the right kind, Cooler pushes the bottle away peevishly.

I wipe the mess off Cooler and try again with Phrag, who's reaching over his brother for the bottle. I'm careful to keep him upright, not on his back. Bottle feeding is tricky. I know from experience about aspiration pneumonia. My guts clench. I don't want that to happen again. So many things can go wrong. The nipple has to be the right size or they'll get too much. You have to go slow and be patient, never force it. The kits could suck formula into their lungs and die — all because I'm trying to help.

Phrag chatters in excitement, grabbing and sucking with great enthusiasm. But then his mouth fills too fast and he spits up. He waves his little arms around as if he can't figure out if he needs to push it away or pull it in.

In his eagerness for more, he keeps flicking the nipple, squirting formula all over his face and my lap. His grunts of frustration mirror my own.

"It looks like it's too big for his mouth," Aaron observes. "Do you have a smaller one?"

I switch to an eyedropper, but quickly see that'll take hours at this rate. Cooler shoves Phrag out of the way, his impatient cries surprisingly loud. In fact, the beavers haven't stopped yammering this entire time. They go from humming to themselves, to mumbling as if they're having a conversation, sounding like teenagers cursing under their breath.

I try lining up the dropper into Cooler's mouth, but he's too eager. He grabs at it, knocking it off target until he's covered in sticky white formula.

"This isn't working." I pull out Nana's logbooks from the top drawer of my workbench and search for clues on how to feed beaver kits. She had to fill these out when she was a wildlife rehabber. Our clubhouse logbook was inspired by them.

As I leaf through, I toss the iPad I'd taken from the house to Aaron. "Can you research baby beavers?"

"I thought you knew everything about orphans already."

I can't tell if Aaron's being sarcastic, so I ignore him.

"Maybe they're bored and just want to swim or something," Jack suggests.

I take a deep breath. I don't know what to do for them, and I hate this feeling. If I'm a natural like Nana said, shouldn't I know?

I slump back on the wall of the clubhouse and run my hand over Phrag's warm little body. There's no expert here but me. And the most important problem right now is that the kits will die if I can't figure out how to feed them.

I try wiping their bums with a wet face cloth to stimulate them into doing their business like I had to do with the box of kittens. That hadn't been in Nana's logbook — I'd learned it from my rehabber magazines. But it doesn't seem to work for the beavers.

Cooler mutters indignantly and pushes me away from his tail. And Phrag just tries to hold my hand with his soft little fingers grabbing and wrapping around mine.

The kits are sticky from the formula. I have to do *something*. I grab the hose from outside and fill a green Rubbermaid tub to wash them. Jack helps me place the kits into the water. They both start crying so loud, I think the neighbors down the lake will hear them. And then it happens. They poop.

"Look at that," I say. "They need water to do their business! I should've known that."

Phrag is frantically swimming after my hand,

emitting a distressed moan. Cooler tries to jump out using Phrag as a ladder.

"They don't seem to like swimming," Jack observes. "I thought all beavers liked water."

"Their house was dry," I say, pulling the kits out of the tub. "Maybe they don't like getting wet." I set them on a bag of wood shavings.

Cooler babbles while I pat his head with a towel. His fur is all spiky as he shakes himself. He starts rubbing along the base of his tail, then rubbing his hands through his fur. He seems intent on grooming every part of himself, even reaching around to get to the fur on his back. With his hand on his hip, he looks like he's doing a mambo dance. He reaches for the other side of his back, balancing on his tail, and falls over.

When I laugh, Cooler gives me a look so full of offense, it doesn't take a whisperer to know that beavers do not like to be laughed at.

Picking up Nana's logbook again, I leaf through desperately. I have a lot to learn about beavers.

"Beavers go to the bathroom in the water," Aaron says, finally looking up from the iPad.

"You're supposed to be telling me things I *don't* know."

"They also rid themselves of a secretion from the castor glands called castoreum in the water so it doesn't attract predators on land," Aaron reads. "Smart. Maybe that's why they don't smell bad. I'd thought they'd stink."

I run a hand over Cooler's back and the kit grabs my finger to shove it into his mouth. Even though he has teeth, he doesn't use them to bite. I know he won't bite, because he's not feeling threatened.

He's just hungry.

# 8

**"WE NEED TO GET GOING," JACK SAYS,**
collecting the notes he'd been working on.

"Where?" I ask, but knowing Jack and his obsession
with being a game warden, I can already guess.

"Duh! To the scene of the crime! We have to start
the investigation before the trail goes cold. Don't you
want to figure out who did this?"

I look at Phrag and Cooler, both busy grooming
themselves. They run their hands near their tails, then
rub every part of their fur, face, and even their arm-
pits like a person having a shower. Though they don't
quite smell shower fresh, whatever it is they're rubbing
through their fur has a mild, sweet odor. Their faces are
set with concentration. This is serious business.

I think of how they're orphans now, with only me to

care for them. Who will show them how to cut down a tree without it falling on their head? How to make a house of sticks, and swim, and . . . do other beaver things? They should be living happy in their lodge with a family who knows what they're doing. Anger surges through me quick and sharp. Some dumb person shot their parents and changed their world.

"Yeah, I want whoever did this to get caught. But we can't leave the kits. They need feeding every four hours. I'm going to make up a schedule so we can take turns."

"I can't take a turn!" Jack says. "Lid and I have to track the poacher!"

He pauses as we all hear gravel crunching on the driveway.

"My parents are home! Quick! Hide the beavers!"

I grab a cardboard box and line it with wood chips and the brown towel. After wrapping the hot water bottle in a dry rag, I stuff it underneath my old teddy bear and place it in the box before lowering the kits inside.

"But, your parents never come in here," Aaron points out.

"That was before Mom found out about the cat."

Whenever kids are doing something they're not supposed to, adults tend to suddenly find us interesting.

"We should go talk to them, to make sure they don't come in." I survey the box and pause. "You think the kits might feel trapped in there? What if they need to get out to use the bathroom?"

I know from experience that baby animals have an instinct. They almost never go in their beds.

Jack uses the box cutter from the workbench and cuts out a door opening on the side of the box. "How's that?"

I look it over. "Better. But now it needs to be hidden."

I find my largest box and tip it sideways. Then I put the bed box inside it and the tub of water, and close the flaps so no one can see inside. Now they're secure. The beavers must be asleep already, because they're quiet.

We head out to face my parents. They're unloading groceries from the car.

"What on earth?" Mom says when she sees me.

I look down at myself and remember the mud and how my tank used to be yellow.

"What have you got all over your face?"

"We were just playing," I say, wiping off the drying grit.

Mom presses her lips together but doesn't say anything. Everyone grabs grocery bags and hauls them into the kitchen.

"Seems like you've got enough helpers," Dad says to Mom. "Going to catch the end of the game." He wanders toward the living room, but stops to tweak my nose, the same way he's done my whole life.

I bat his hand away. *"Dad!"*

"Can't help it," he throws over his shoulder.

"Popsicles!" Jack says, pulling the box out of a grocery bag.

Mom takes the box from him and stashes them in the back of the freezer. "Not before dinner." She bends to place a tub of yogurt onto a shelf. "What have you three been up to besides playing in the mud?"

"Nothing," I say. Too fast.

Mom looks up suspiciously. I search for something quick. "We were helping Jack train Lid to do a track. We run and hide and then Lid finds us. We were just leaving to go finish the game."

Jack breaks into a grin.

"Sounds like fun," Mom says, shutting the fridge. "Be home for dinner. Your dad's shift starts tomorrow."

Dad's a traveling nurse, working two weeks away from home, then staying home for two. Normally I hate when he starts a new shift, but right now the timing works out. That means it's mostly just my sister and me at home.

On our way out, I find Marley draped over a chair in the den.

"'Sup, mongrels?" she says.

"We were wondering if you could meet us in the clubhouse to show us how to fill out our logbook properly. I mean, do you write the stuff you're *going* to have a meeting about first, or do you write it after?"

Marley snorts. "I wouldn't go in there if you paid me. It smells like a barn inside a boys' locker room next to a monkey factory."

As we head to the boat, I congratulate myself on my genius method of guaranteeing my sister won't go snooping. For now, the kits are safe from being found.

# 9

I CUT THE MOTOR NEAR WHERE WE'D
seen the dead adult beavers.

We drift to the bank. I don't want to look, but Jack
somehow finds them right away while I secure the boat.

"They've been shot!" Jack says. "Look at the hole."

Despite myself, I peer over his shoulder as he
crouches next to the sleek carcasses.

"That means maybe we can find the shell casings!"
Jack jumps up. "Come on, Lid."

I didn't think Lid knew how to find shell casings,
but he seems to be searching for something. We walk
the shoreline of the channel between Lake Little Hawk
and Lake Wild, Lid's nose to the ground. His expression is intense as he zigzags over fallen logs and tracks
through mud.

A hot summer wind blows in our faces, bringing the smell of earthy, damp bog. Lid throws his nose in the air and closes his eyes. I stop too when I notice the sun is warming my right shoulder. How did it get so low? We don't have much time before dinner.

"Maybe we should come back tomorrow," Aaron says, seeming to read my mind.

"The evidence could be gone by then," Jack says. The look on his face is just as intense as his dog's.

The tall grasses rustle around us, sounding like whispers. Crows caw at us from the bush line, as if accusing us of killing the beavers. The beaver lodge sits in the middle of the channel, silent and empty. A monument to where I could've died. I try to shake off a feeling of foreboding.

Aaron brushes at some burrs stuck to his socks. Back at the clubhouse he'd washed the mud from our ATV disaster off his shoes. He's the only kid I know who insists on shoes instead of sandals in summer. Even though I've told him no one cares about the extra skin between his two toes.

If I had a webbed toe, I'd show it off. I'd tell everyone I was part fish like Aquaman. No, I'd call myself BeaverGirl. Too bad Aaron doesn't see the potential.

Now, in an attempt to keep his shoes clean, Aaron leaps to balance on a stump, his lips pressed together. That boy does not like getting dirty. Even as a kid he'd cry if his hands got sticky. I remember him years ago when we were neighbors, holding out his fingers while his mom washed them off.

Abruptly, I think of the beaver kits holding out their formula-covered fingers. We need to get back in time to feed them again.

Lid stops and paws next to something red in the grasses. We all see the shotgun shells at the same time.

"Good boy!" Jack seems as surprised as the rest of us. He tosses a dog cookie.

Lid snaps it out of the air. While the dog crunches happily, Jack pulls out his "specialized game warden tools," a Ziploc bag and a pair of tweezers. The bag's been labeled with a marker, EVIDENCE KIT. Using the tweezers, Jack picks up the shells and drops them into the bag.

We walk a little farther, avoiding the wet spots between clumps of tall reeds. A blue heron lets out a startled croak, scaring the fluffernutter out of us. It flies away, its long legs dangling. Frogs start to call in earnest as the day winds down, and I feel more and more like an intruder.

Lid's pawing near something else in the mud. I crouch to see a few dirty cigarette butts. "Gross."

"Don't touch them!" Jack vibrates with excitement. "These can break the case wide open! There's a whole episode where a case was solved by getting DNA off a cigarette butt and catching a moose poacher!"

Jack's obsession with everything game warden got serious once Lid arrived. It was also around the time that his dad left, when he needed something else to think about.

He'd researched how game wardens train their detector dogs. They use a toy ball as a reward. Jack improvised with cookies since there isn't much Lid won't do for a cookie.

While Jack's busy telling us about his great knowledge of DNA collection, he fails to watch his dog.

"Er . . ." Aaron says.

"And that's why I use these," Jack continues, holding

up the tweezers and pinching them. "So I don't contaminate the evidence."

"Uh . . . Jack?" I say, pointing.

Jack whirls around in time to see Lid hoover up the last butt.

"No! Drop it!" Jack crams his hand down Lid's throat, but comes up holding nothing but slobber.

"That's just great," Jack says, while Aaron and I try not to crack up. Lid folds his ears out sideways, looking pleased with himself.

"At least you have the shells," I say. "What will those tell us?"

Jack studies his Ziploc bag. "We know now that the shooter stood right here and shot the beavers."

He stands on the spot and aims a pretend shotgun, mimicking the crime. Then he looks around, deep in thought. "Maybe we should go to Dillon's Hardware and see if they'll tell us who bought ammo lately. It's worth—"

Lid gives a short, high-pitched bark. The dog glances briefly back at us before bolting into the trees.

We look at each other, then charge after him.

# 10

"HE'S GOT A TRACK," JACK YELLS OVER his shoulder.

I didn't lie to Mom earlier. Jack applies the detector dog training techniques that he learned, and we help by hiding so Lid can practice finding us. And right before he finds us, he usually barks just like how he sounds now.

Lid's black tail wags above the grasses, giving us something to follow. We race into the brush till we come out on a trail.

"Wait for us, Lid!" Jack calls.

A flagging tail up ahead turns off onto a smaller path. In our haste not to lose sight of Lid, we crash headlong into a mean raspberry bush, the prickles shredding our exposed arms and legs. Jack and Aaron howl. They get tangled in each other and have a quick shoving argument. Aaron never wins that one.

The lengthening shadows are getting longer by the minute. If we don't hurry, we'll miss dinner. But even more urgent — the beavers need *their* dinner. "We don't have time for this," I say, following Lid.

And then we burst out of the bushes and find ourselves on someone's fancy lawn. It stretches down to a lake. When I see the house, I recognize that we're in a bay of my own lake. This is Mr. Kang's backyard. He owns the florist shop in town and also works as a landscaper. His home and property are always perfect.

"Look!" Aaron points to a row of trees lying on the ground.

*Almost* always perfect.

Four ugly tree trunks stick up out of the lawn, sad broken soldiers in a row. They look as though they've been chewed off by a beaver. Their trunks are gnawed around the whole girth of the tree. The gnawing has made the trunk get smaller and smaller until the tree couldn't support the weight and came crashing down. Loose branches and wood chips litter the area like pale teardrops.

"Uh-oh," I say. "You think the beavers cut down Mr. Kang's nice trees? And then he got mad? Mad enough to want revenge?"

Jack tosses another cookie to Lid. "Looks that way. I think we solved the case."

Aaron's studying the trunks, wearing a puzzled expression. "Something's not right."

We take a closer look at the trunks and see lime green paint marks.

"Something bright green's been scraped against the bark," Aaron says, pointing.

And those teeth marks look less like marks made by beaver teeth and more like many small chops from an ax. Were they intended to look like teeth marks?

"What're you kids doing?" A voice calls from the house.

Aaron jumps, grabbing his chest.

"Sorry, Mr. Kang," I call up to the figure standing on the deck. "We noticed you've had some trouble with beavers."

"What?" Mr. Kang yells down at us. "Is that you? Ron Lewis's girl?"

"Madison," I say.

"If you think those were cut by beavers, you need glasses more than me!"

"Do you own a shotgun?" Jack yells back. "'Cause we've got two murdered beavers and some strong evidence that the game wardens are going to find interesting."

Aaron slaps his face with both hands and drags them down his cheeks, pulling his eyes long. "We're in so much trouble," he moans.

I'm as surprised as Aaron about Jack's sass. But when he uses that voice around grownups, it almost sounds like he knows what he's talking about. It's possible he's feeling brave because Mr. Kang is so far away.

Mr. Kang scratches his head in astonishment and opens his mouth a few times. "Before you start accusing me of . . . whatever you're trying to say, young man, I think you should start by looking into the meetings going on down at the hardware store."

Lid throws himself onto a pile of goose poop and rolls, flashing an upside-down smile of ecstasy.

"What meetings?" Jack asks.

"Exactly," Mr. Kang says.

BY THE TIME WE GET BACK, IT'S DEFI-
nitely after dinner.

The boat coasts through the surface of the water
before it lightly bumps our dock, sending out quiet ripples that reflect a mix of pink and purple.

"We are so grounded," Aaron says, eyeing the dusky
sky.

I take a look at us, caked in dried mud and blood
and scratches as though we've been attacked by a herd
of cats. Me with muck still in my hair. At least it's not
goose poop. I glance at Lid's smeared neck.

I'd called home to say we'd lost track of time. As
long as I call, Mom tends not to have any meltdowns.
But she would've called Aaron's mom to tell her when

to pick him up, and I'll bet that his mom was currently having said meltdown.

Aaron's parents are stricter than mine or Jack's. Probably because they're home more. Aaron always tells Jack he's lucky his dad lives three hours away. But I don't think Jack feels lucky.

We head straight to the clubhouse. That's when I know I really am in serious trouble. I pick up the note taped to the kits' cardboard box.

*You're in serious trouble.*

Panic stops my heart for a moment until I look closer at the note. This isn't Mom's handwriting. *Marley.*

I cringe, but it's better than Mom. Maybe my sister hasn't told on me yet.

Noises from the box cut my thoughts short. Someone's awake and starting to become unhappy.

Aaron opens the flaps of the large box and we peer in. The beavers blink out at us. And then Phrag holds up little arms toward me like Jack's sister, Lorrie, when she squeals, "Uppy, uppy!"

"We should feed them again before we go in," I say.

"My mom's likely on her way now," Aaron says, "but let's stay in here while we wait."

58

I mix another bottle of formula and we proceed with a repeat of the first feeding. The contents of the bottle spill everywhere and the beavers grow more frustrated by the second. How am I going to get enough food into them to keep them from starving to death?

"So what d'you think Mr. Kang was talking about?" Aaron asks Jack as he meticulously plucks off tiny black spines from a bush stuck to the waistband of his shorts.

Phrag wheezes and huffs on my lap, slapping the bottle away.

"I don't know. But secret meetings sound like something we should find out. Let's get together on Dillon Street in the morning."

"If I'm not grounded," Aaron says.

Cooler grabs the hem of my shirt and sucks at a spot where formula had spilled. I think of the teeth I'd felt when he'd sucked my finger.

"Maybe they're old enough to eat soft food. Too bad we don't have bread. I could make formula French toast." Nana had called it that. I remember the first time getting excited because I loved French toast, but instead of dipping bread in milk and egg and slathering it with maple syrup, she soaked pieces of bread in formula and fed it to baby raccoons.

Aaron rummages in his pack and pulls out a squashed peanut butter sandwich.

"What . . . How long has *that* been in there?"

He shrugs his bony shoulders. "Just remembered it. You want it or not?"

I scrape the peanut butter off one side and pull out one of my feeding pans. Dumping the formula into the pan, I sop it up with the bread and break it into tiny pieces.

The kits investigate, mumbling and holding the bread in their little fingers. Phrag delicately taps his nose with it before tasting. They quickly get the hang of eating it and grab more, swirling the bread around in their hands like eating corn on the cob. They don't stop talking about it the whole time.

*Nom, nom, nom, nummy, nummy, nom.*

I breathe a relieved sigh.

Through it all, Phrag still wants to hold my hand, his tiny fingers covered in a glue-like paste. I can tell when Cooler's eaten enough once he starts using the mush to spread on the side of their cardboard house. He carries the mush, clutching it to his chest, and then pats his box as though laying down cement.

We're all interrupted by the sound of a vehicle pulling up.

"That's our ride," Aaron says, standing with Jack.

"Stakeout, tomorrow," Jack says. "Don't forget."

"It'll have to be a fast stakeout," I say as I open the door, following them out.

We all freeze in our tracks. Aaron makes a sound like he's swallowed a bug. Marley's waiting with her arms crossed. I'd nearly forgotten the note. Aaron and Jack inch around her and run toward the Jeep like cowards.

"I thought you said it smelled in here and you'd never come in?" I say casually.

"Of course I went in. After you so obviously wanted me to stay out. You think I wouldn't recognize reverse psychology when I see it? I *invented* it."

My sister is a worthier adversary than I give her credit for.

"So what do you want? There's nothing in here." I

cling to the shred of hope that she hasn't actually seen the kits.

"Let's discuss the *rodents* you currently have stashed when you weren't supposed to bring home any more rescues."

## 12

MARLEY ENJOYED WATCHING ME SQUIRM all evening.

But dinner ended, then family movie night ended, and still Marley hadn't said anything.

Now I'm in bed researching beavers on my iPad. One thing's for sure: It takes time to rehab beavers. They need more than the usual food and water. They also require their social needs met as part of their total care.

A beaver's family ties are so important that they're born with strong instincts for building bonds. A family lives together in a small house underneath the ice all through the winter. They have to get along.

It's not as though they can escape to the den if their sister is poking them with her gunky toenail clippings.

And in the summer, they have to look out for each other, slapping their tails to tell the rest of the family if there's danger.

They actually need hugs and cuddles as much as they need food and water. Any other wild animal, Nana kept telling me, needs the opposite. You don't pet or cuddle animals that you're trying to help. They aren't pets. The whole point of rehabbing animals is to care for them so they can be released back in the wild. If they're too used to humans, they won't be able to live normally anymore. They don't like being touched, either — sometimes they even die from fright.

But beavers *want* to be groomed and be kept company. Beavers like to be fussed over and socialized so that they'll develop into well-rounded members of a family. Basically, they need to be loved.

And since these two are orphans, all that attention is going to have to come from me.

These kits are different from any other animals I've researched. And if I'm honest, I'm surprised how quickly my feelings for them have grown. Already, I feel the kits inside my heart.

A soft knock on my door.

"Yeah?" I close the page about beaver kit diets.

Mom comes in. "Thought you might be asleep. It's late—what are you doing still up?" She sits on my bed.

"Going over some planning. I'm too excited to sleep."

"Ah." She glances at my autographed poster of Jane Goodall over my bed. "Trip's coming up soon. What are you most excited about? The hotel? The food? The museum?"

"You know."

Mom grins, then she straightens and a serious expression comes over her. "I'm so proud of you and your sister. Your dad and I have been more absent lately. I know that. But it's nice that you two are responsible young ladies who we can trust. I'm hoping things will slow down at work soon. But tomorrow I have to go in early again, and Dad leaves for Clearwater, so we won't be here when you get up. I'm sorry, hon."

Sometimes it makes me sad when there's no one around when I wake up. But not tonight. "That's okay, Mom. I know what it's like to have goals."

She laughs and shakes her head, standing. "How did I get so lucky? G'night, Mad. See you tomorrow night."

• • •

I'm almost asleep when I feel a hand clamp over my mouth and another plug my nose.

I fight like a rabid badger, arms and legs everywhere.

Marley removes her hands and smirks at me. "Settle down!" she whispers.

"Are you trying to kill me?" I suck in and out, holding my chest.

"I just didn't want you to scream. Holy drama."

"Right. Not breathing isn't scary at all. Good choice." My oxygen levels return to normal as I glare. "What do you want?"

"We need to finish our discussion."

My stomach plummets. I lean against my headboard and wait for her to get to the point.

"So." She flops on my bed. "I'm willing to keep your little secret."

"And in exchange . . ."

"I'm having Cal over next Friday. With a few other friends. Mom and Dad don't need to know."

Ah. So there it is. She's probably been waiting for just such an opportunity. With Mom going to Boston next week and Dad still gone on shift, that means we'll be alone all night. Marley's in charge. It's as if our parents have never met her. Don't they know she'll want to have a party or have her boyfriend come over? This is *Marley*. Never mind. It works for me.

# 13

FIRST THING THE NEXT MORNING, I GO
out to check on the kits.

When I get to the door of the clubhouse, I can't
open it. Something's jamming the door from behind. I
push it open a crack and then shove my way in. There's
a scraping noise as something shifts and falls behind it.
Once I get into the shed, I gape.

*What the—?*

A tidal wave of garden tools that had once been
neatly shelved is now stacked up behind the door and
piled around the beavers' box. Tomato cages, seed pack-
ets, a wicked-looking tool with a wooden handle and
three metal prongs, plastic planters, a mini trowel, and
a few rows of decorative garden edging. Even some of
my rehabber tools are shoved into a corner. Empty food

pans scatter the floor. Basically, anything in the shed that wasn't too heavy has been moved.

Worst of all is an old bag of bedding soil that's been tipped over, mixed with the water in the pan, and spread out over the floor and walls.

And in the center of it sit two satisfied-looking beaver kits. They're grooming themselves, but when they see me, they both immediately waddle toward me. As if they have no idea how this mess happened. They'd just woken up to a destroyed clubhouse.

"Did you two work all night?"

Their box has been thoroughly chewed and leans sadly to the left, with items propped against it. A pair of gloves is stuffed into the door hole along with some kind of book. I lean in and recognize the logbook.

"Hey!" I step forward to rescue the book, but trip over a pair of pruning shears. One of the telescoping handles extends out to bash me in the shin.

Phrag scratches at my leg, trying to climb. Cooler glares at me and curses. They definitely have distinct personalities.

I don't have their breakfast, because I'd been so eager

to check on them. But clearly they need food right now. They also need attention. I look around at the chaos. I don't have time to clean it up. I have to get them fed before I meet up with the guys in town.

"Okay, you win," I say, grabbing their formula. "You're coming with me." It'll save me a trip getting them food. And since Marley and I have the house to ourselves, I don't see why I can't.

My sister's staring at her phone like a zombie while eating cereal when I come in carrying the kits. She doesn't even notice as I shuffle down the hall with them toward the bathroom. I start the tub and leave them on the floor while I go to fix their breakfast.

After my research, I know I can introduce yogurt, fresh herbs, slices of peaches, and some canned sweet potato along with their formula French toast. Luckily, Mom just stocked up. I put it all on a tray. Marley watches me carry it out of the kitchen without comment.

Once I lower the tray to the tiled floor, the celebration starts. The kits investigate the new food. They stuff the French toast in their mouths first, then cautiously taste the rest. Cooler pats the sweet potato as though considering how to use it as building material. Phrag squeaks with excitement over the peaches. They generally have a party at every meal, stuffing food into their mouths with their busy little fingers, grunting and moaning. They garble their delight to each other and then to me, eating and talking at the same time. Phrag reaches his sticky hand to grab mine.

Once they've eaten, I lower them in for a bath to do their business. They aren't quite as panicked as last time. Phrag chases around after my hand at first. Cooler swims the length of the tub, investigating. They start enjoying themselves, circling the edge like two fuzzy sharks, their webbed back feet paddling underneath them. But with all his kicking, Cooler accidentally pulls the plug.

*Pandemonium!*

The minute the kits hear the water gurgling down the drain, they go into hysterics, splashing frantically and swimming back and forth. Cooler finds the source of the water leak and tries shoving his hands over the drain hole. Then he grabs the bar of soap to use as a plug. A shampoo bottle. The back scrubber. When nothing works, he grabs his brother and tries stuffing Phrag into the hole.

Phrag seriously opposes being used as a stopper, if his high-pitched complaints are any indication.

Marley pops the door open and takes in the scene. Yogurt footprints all over the floor. Me, soaking wet and sticky with peach juice, kneeling next to the tub. Cooler stuffing a wailing Phrag into the drain.

Marley's expression doesn't change.

"It's for you," she says casually, handing me the phone. Then she shuts the door.

"Madi?" Jack's voice.

"Kinda busy right now, Jack . . ."

"It's the beavers," he says. "There's been another murder."

# 14

"SO HERE'S WHAT WE KNOW," JACK says.

We're outside Dillon's Hardware. Normally at this time of day I'm doing my observations. Watching wildlife in its natural environment and quietly taking notes. It's what Jane Goodall did when she made all her groundbreaking discoveries about chimps. But my whole routine has been upended since the kits arrived.

While Jack updates us on his findings from his investigation so far, Lid sits next to us on the sidewalk and licks his butt with dedication.

"The Township's had flooding problems, right? I mean, we saw Birch Street. The beavers are blocking drainage culverts by building dams inside them. And that makes the roads flood. But not just roads—there's whole fields out behind Dillon's that are covered in water. So the Township tried to get rid of the problem by *drowning* a beaver in a trap!"

Aaron and I both gasp.

"How do you know these things?" Aaron asks. He's got leftover jam on his cheek, which isn't like him. He must've been in a hurry this morning too.

"Confidential informant," Jack says with a raised eyebrow.

I raise an eyebrow back.

Lid's brows waggle one at a time as his gaze bounces between us.

Jack continues in his sleuth voice, "Anyway. When people found out—I mean, that part's been on TV —the council got hundreds of calls and letters of complaint. People were outraged. Now the Township doesn't want anything to do with killing beavers. It's bad for their image. They've just been letting the beavers dam things up."

"So then what's the part about more beavers getting killed?" I ask.

"That's the thing. Someone reported a beaver shot out near Birch Street yesterday. Same way the kits' parents were killed."

"If more adults are being shot," I say, "then any of them could have orphaned kits."

I think about that. What if the beaver from Birch Street had kits? Helpless kits right now sitting in their beaver lodge, waiting for their parents to return. Were there more orphans out there? How many more beaver parents will be killed? I feel sick.

"This is a disaster," I say.

"We have to find the killers and stop them," Aaron agrees.

Lid abruptly notices the jam. While Aaron speaks, the dog leans in. "They aren't going to—" Lid's tongue misses and slips inside Aaron's mouth. "Gaaack!" Aaron starts spitting.

"Dude!" Jack says, with a grossed-out grin. "Do you know where that tongue's been?"

"I *know!* I think I tasted it." Now Aaron looks as sick as I feel. He feverishly wipes at his mouth.

Again, it's up to me to keep the boys focused. "So

why are we here, exactly?" I ask Jack, indicating the store.

"Remember Mr. Kang told us about secret meetings?"

"Town council meetings?" Aaron says, still glaring at Lid. "At the hardware store? That doesn't make sense."

"We're about to find out," Jack says. "I'm going to see what I can learn about this." He holds up his evidence bag with the shotgun shells. "You two mingle." He motions for us to follow, and we all troop into the store.

Aaron and I wander down an aisle that has big spools of some kind of wire. Dillon's Hardware always smells like dust and rotten wood and some other weird metallic odor that I don't like.

A group of old men in the other aisle are talking. I hear the word "beavers" and perk up. Aaron nods at me and we hide behind the spools of wire to listen.

"The Township won't do it, Jim. I'm telling you, the landowners have to take matters into their own hands."

"They built a dam right in my field where my crops are growing!" another voice says. "I've spent years draining my land to make it productive. It's so frustrating."

"They're a rodent, like rats," the first voice says. "They're pests, and what do you do with pests?"

"Dynamite and destroying the dams doesn't work. You know a family of them can rebuild a dam overnight."

"That's what I've been saying. The only way to go after them is put a bounty on them. The council will see reason."

*A bounty?* The Township would pay for every dead beaver? No, Jack just said they don't want bad publicity. But would these men talk the council into it?

A steamy volcano bubbles up inside me. I start marching toward them until Aaron drags me back.

"That's not going to solve anything," he whispers, pulling me out of the store where Jack and Lid are waiting.

"I found out something interesting," Jack says, jiggling the bag. "When I asked the clerk if anyone bought these recently, he laughed and said pretty much every landowner in Willow Grove. He said they'd declared war on the beavers."

He stuffs the evidence in his pocket and adds smugly, "I told you these shells would work. What did *you* hear?"

Aaron and I glance at each other. "The same," I say.

Jack looks a little crestfallen, but nods. "We need a plan." He eyes us knowingly. "Sounds like it's up to us to find the poacher."

"Before they get a bounty put on beavers," Aaron says.

"A *bounty?*" Jack asks, eyes wide. "Then anyone can kill more beavers and it won't be illegal. There'll be no crime to solve." He deflates.

"There isn't any bounty yet," I say, burning with the need to do something. "So we're not too late to stop it. Let's go!"

# 15

I SPIN AROUND AND RUN.

Lid bounds ahead.

"Where we going?" Jack asks, feet pounding the sidewalk behind me.

I point to the Township office at the end of the street. When we burst through the doors, the air conditioning hits me in the face.

A lady with soft blond curls looks up from her computer. "I'm sorry, no dogs allowed." She points to the sign.

Jack *tsk*s and pushes Lid back out. Lid stares through the windows with an incredulous expression, as if he can't believe there'd be such a ridiculous rule.

"Can I help you?" The lady comes to the counter. Her nametag says CARRIE.

"We've got new information about your beaver problem," I say.

"We don't have a beaver problem," Carrie says, unconvincingly.

As we tell Carrie about the landowners and what they plan to do, it occurs to me that I have to be very careful. If anyone from the Township knew I had orphaned beaver kits at home, they'd take them away in a hurry. And then what would they do with them? There aren't any licensed rehabbers around here since Nana. They'd have to take them far away. Or worse, decide it's too much bother. It would be easier to just release the kits so they don't have to deal with them.

But Phrag and Cooler are too young to survive on their own. Kits stay with their families for two years.

Carrie lets out a small sigh. "If the council decides that a bounty is what they should do to control the population, then it's for the best. They have wildlife experts to consult with. They know what they're doing. You can trust that they'll deal with the matter in the correct way."

I have a bad feeling. It sounds like a quiet solution to the Township's problem would be to just let the landowners deal with things their way. I'm pretty sure no one will care about beavers dying as long as there's a flooding problem.

"But, the *beavers*," Aaron says. He's coming to the same conclusions as I am—I see it in his face. "You should meet them. They have these fingers . . . and they *talk* . . . and they're nice, and . . . and they're all going to die."

Aaron's so smart when he's not around strangers. I shoot him a warning look as he scrambles to explain.

"Madi will tell you. She's an animal whisperer."

*Uh-oh.*

Carrie turns to me. "What's an animal whisperer?"

I shift my feet. "Um . . . it's just an interest of mine. My nana was an animal whisperer and she taught me how to listen to wildlife. I'm going to save animals like Jane Goodall. When I'm older, of course."

"Well, that sounds like a wonderful goal. I wish more people cared to learn how to listen to animals."

I let out a tiny breath, the tension in my shoulders relaxing a bit. She doesn't have that knowing look that most adults give kids when they don't believe them. She's really listening to me.

"Now. All of you should stop worrying about this

and spend your summer doing something fun. You've got the whole outside to play in. Go be kids!"

So much for listening.

I glance at Jack and Aaron and we have a conversation with our eyes. We leave, more subdued than when we came in.

Outside, Jack kicks a rock. "I can't believe no one cares about beaver poaching."

We're silent as we think about what to do next. A truck goes past with a pile of trees in the back.

Jack perks up. "Wait a minute. Mr. Kang."

"What about him?" I say.

"Someone went on his private property and destroyed his trees. Still a mystery *why* they cut his trees," he adds to himself. "But that's against the law. You can't just cut down someone else's trees. So we have to solve who did."

"It's more important to figure out who killed the beavers," I say.

"It's the same thing," Jack says. "Because Lid did the track. You both saw it. We followed the scent trail directly from where the shooter killed the beavers. It led right to Mr. Kang's trees. That means whoever shot

Phrag and Cooler's parents is the same person who cut the trees."

"How do you know for sure?" Aaron says. "Lid could've just been going for a walk for all you know."

"No way. You heard him. Lid was on a track. He linked the murder with the tree cutter. And I know Mr. Kang's pretty upset about his trees. Someone will care who destroyed them. If we solve that crime, we solve the beaver-killing crime at the same time."

"Okay, so how do we solve it?" Aaron asks, always the logical one.

"I have to think on it," Jack says, looking uncertain.

But the start of an idea is niggling at me. Something about the way Phrag and Cooler reacted this morning in the tub. When they heard the water draining, they'd freaked out. The animal whisperer part of my brain buzzes.

"I think I have a plan," I say.

# 16

AFTER THE DISAPPOINTING TOWNSHIP
office visit, we split up for the day.

Aaron had something to do with his family. Jack
said he and Lid would *investigate*. I fed the kits, changed
their water, and did more beaver research until Mom
came home for supper.

Afterward I convinced her that I had to go do my
observations before the end of the day since I'd missed
them that morning.

I take the ATV back to Birch Street. Beavers work at
dusk, and I think I know where to find them.

I started observations once I learned how Jane
Goodall would go out every day and sit and watch wild
animals to understand how animals act normally. I've
learned a lot about the habits of raccoons, ducks, rabbits,

skunks, crows, and deer, and once even a fox hunting mice. But beavers are nocturnal — they do most of their activity at night. I haven't observed them much.

I park the ATV and follow Birch Creek on foot until I come to a beaver dam stretched across the narrowest part. Climbing on the dam, I pull out a few sticks and shove a big log out of the way until water starts to flow through again.

Then I set myself up next to some trees to wait. If these beavers are anything like Phrag and Cooler, they're going to come to the sound of the water.

I lay out my things around me so I don't have to move much. That's key for observing without disturbing the animals. If you sit very still, they'll ignore you. Or in Jane Goodall's case, climb all over you. My water bottle is on my left. My logbook's on my right, and my binoculars I keep around my neck.

While I wait for the beavers to show, I watch a squirrel. He's so busy carrying pine nuts around and finding places to bury them, he doesn't take notice of me. His tiny paws dig furiously through the leaf litter on the ground. Once he's dug a hole, he drops the nut in and shoves the dirt over top of it. Satisfied, he whirls around and runs straight over my shoe on his way to find more pinecones.

My left leg starts to get pins and needles. I shift slightly and the squirrel disappears into the bushes.

Without the rustling of the squirrel, the quiet of the woods descends. When I sit like this, one of my favorite things about being here besides watching the animals is the stillness. It's peaceful in the woods alone.

I feel the coolness of the forest being released into the summer air. The sharp scent of trees surrounds me. I smell bark and green leaves and sun-heated needles and rotting leaves on the ground. The moss by my shoes has been kicked up. I like the earthy smell of that, too.

I notice the difference from morning. The smells are more pungent. It's quieter without so many bird calls. There's a calm settling in and filling me up.

A mosquito buzzes in my ear and I try to remain still and not swat it. I hope the beavers hurry up. I don't have much time before I have to go.

That's when I notice the sleek brown head watching me from the surface of the creek.

We lock into a staring contest until the beaver seems to decide I'm not worth worrying about. He turns and makes his way to the dam. When he climbs out of the water and shakes, I see how huge he is. I can't imagine little Phrag and Cooler growing up to be this size — as big as Lid, but with shorter legs.

The beaver studies the damage I did to his dam, pushes at the log, and seems to think about how to fix it. Then he slides back into the water. Another head appears, carrying a long stick. That beaver shoves his stick into the dam, jiggling it to make it fit.

The first beaver comes back clutching mud to his chest. He waddles carefully, upright on his back feet, looking like a hunched-over old man carrying parcels. He's muttering to the other beaver.

The beavers work together, going and collecting sticks and pulling up mud from the bottom of the creek. I jot notes in the logbook as I watch them patch up the dam. They pat mud in place just the way I'd seen Cooler do on his box.

I think of the kits I have hidden at home with their funny habits and separate personalities. The more I get to know them, the more urgent it feels that no more beavers die.

• • •

The next day I head to the boat launch with the boat to pick up Jack and Aaron.

"So are you going to tell us this plan of yours now?" Aaron asks.

"I'm still working on it," I say. "First we need to get to the channel."

The boys settle into their usual seats, Lid hogging the bow, ready to catch the wind in his ears. I brace my feet on the back transom and grab the pull start. Sometimes this part's tricky.

*Vrrrooom!* The motor jumps to life.

We putter across the bay. The motor's only a four-horse after all. Morning sun dances off the ripples on the water like fireflies. I forgot my hat again so it also beats on my head. The wind in my face feels good.

I think about what Carrie from the Township said about us just being kids and enjoying our summer. We used to do that, back when Jack and Aaron lived next door. We grew up together, catching frogs and having races over our beach all day.

Aaron's always been obsessed with engineering, building complicated sandcastle villages. Back then, Marley used to play with us too, helping us make moats and dams. We'd build a network of trenches and bridges and then pour buckets of water down it. We'd watch the water follow the channels until the cascade would wash everything away down to the lake.

Then Marley grew into a teenager and wanted nothing to do with us. With me.

Aaron moved away first, into town after his mom quit her job at the bank. Then Jack's mom wanted a bigger family and they moved into that huge house on Lake Little Hawk. Now, with Jack's dad gone, they might have to change back to a smaller house. Maybe we'll be neighbors again.

Once I turned twelve, I was allowed to use the boat and ATV to go see my friends. That was my excuse.

But we don't have time for frog races anymore. How can we, when we know about the beaver situation? No one else in this town's going to care about beavers being killed. It really is up to us.

I slow down once we arrive at the mouth of the channel. The small wash from our wake pushes us further in toward a weed bed.

"What are we doing, Madi?" Aaron asks again.

"We need to collect food for the kits."

"You think they'll eat wood now?" Jack asks.

"They don't eat wood. They eat bark off young saplings. But their favorite is usually food that they've grown up with. This channel is full of water lilies. They eat the roots of water vegetation, so we're going to collect them. And we also have to get them some building material."

"You want them to build a lodge?" Aaron asks, perking up.

"Not quite," I say.

# 17

MARLEY'S BOYFRIEND, CAL, SHOWS UP just as we're hauling our tangled forest of branches to the clubhouse.

She's taking full advantage of our secrecy pact by having a boy over when Mom's not home. She knows I can't tell.

Cal steps out of his truck wearing board shorts, work boots, a plaid shirt with the sleeves ripped off, and a straw cowboy hat. I remember Marley told our parents he works on his dad's farm. I have to admit I see why Marley thinks he's cute.

"Planning a really big bonfire?" he asks, giving me a lopsided grin.

"That's right." I think fast. "For the party on Friday."

Cal watches Aaron drag a branch taller than he is. Though most things are taller than Aaron.

"Just a suggestion," Cal says. "You might want to collect *dead* wood. It burns better."

"*Oh!*" I say, to humor him. I stand in front of the soggy water lilies I'd dropped. "Good tip, thanks."

Marley appears at the side door. "Hey. You should come in. We've been having a rodent problem out there."

"What?" Cal looks around in alarm. "You have rats?"

"Big ones." Marley indicates how large with a surprisingly accurate depiction.

"Whoa. You kids be careful out there." He tucks a strand of sandy hair behind his ear and gives me a wink. He's much nicer than her last boyfriend.

As they go in, Marley casts me a look over her shoulder. Loosely translated to mean *Death if you tell.*

We spend the rest of the day transforming the clubhouse into a beaver habitat.

Well, Aaron and I do. Jack keeps busy plotting his investigation.

"Listen," he says, holding up a list. "Yesterday I did some recon at the store."

"What?" I ask.

"*Recon*. It means I hid near the checkout counter and took down the names of everyone who bought ammo." He seems proud to tell us. I suppose it's the same as what I did last night. Observation.

"And I think I have a prime suspect." He circles a name on the list. "Mr. Archer."

"Holly's dad?" Aaron asks. Then his face lights up. "Holly lives on Birch Street!"

"Exactly!" Jack says. They smack hands so loud, it startles Lid, who's busy cleaning my food trays with his tongue. At least it keeps his attention away from the kits. He's ignored them since that first day.

"So what if he lives on Birch Street?" I say.

"I don't think it's a coincidence that the last beaver to be shot was on the same street as someone who lives there and who bought ammo."

I leave Jack to his planning and get Aaron to help me with my old kiddie pool from our garage. We cram it inside, folding it in half to stuff it through the door. It takes up half of the shed.

"Now we need to build platforms," I say, "so the kits can climb in and out of the pool themselves."

We use pieces of old planks we find behind the shed. They work like a kind of sidewalk with a wheelchair ramp along one full side of the pool. Inside the pool I place a few pieces of board so the kits can slide in and climb out.

Next we drag in our pile of sticks, willow branches, and lily roots. The branches make horrid screeching sounds on the tin door as we shove them inside. The lily roots were tricky to pull out of the muck while hanging upside down out of a boat. I hope the kits don't go through these too fast, but I have a feeling I'll be doing it every day to get them fresh food. Beavers are a lot more work than I thought.

Phrag and Cooler inspect everything with glee. Turning things over in their hands, tasting, muttering their opinions, twirling the willow twigs and peeling the bark off. They hang over the sidewalk and stare solemnly at the empty pool.

We dump the potting soil next to the sticks and then I go out to get the hose. All that's left now for step one of my plan is to fill the pool.

When I come back inside, the kits are arguing over a stick. It must be an excellent piece because the fight's getting ugly. Phrag grunts as he tries to yank the stick from his brother. But Cooler is bigger. He curses right back and holds fast to the stick clutched to his chest. They push and pull each other across the clubhouse.

"I can't think over their racket," Jack says, waving his notepad at the kits. He gets up from the table where it's crammed next to the workbench. "I'll go get us lunch."

Someone's going to hear the kits' squalling. Phrag falls backwards when he loses his grip on the coveted stick. I divert their attention, squeezing the nozzle of the hose. Water gushes into their pool.

I lower the kits in. They swim around, do their business, and then crawl out on their own. I know their routine now. They sit on the sidewalk and groom themselves. A nap will be next.

Jack returns with healthy-looking sandwiches on actual brown bread complete with leafy greens. Marley must've made them. *Huh.* She would never have made them for *me.*

Lid instantly becomes fixated, a string of drool leaking out the side of his lips.

"Can you tell us the plan now, Madi?" Aaron says as he picks up a sandwich. A piece of lettuce drops from his hand and hardly hits the floor before the dog pounces. Lid's satisfied expression gives way to a slow horror. He spits it out, sniffs it cautiously, and then slides Aaron a wounded look, his eyes full of accusation.

I produce the iPod I'd taken from the house. "This is the plan."

Stuffing it into a waterproof Otter bag, I press Play. At the sound of running water, everyone, including Lid, looks at me, puzzled.

"Step two will take some time," I say.

I wait until the kits trundle off to their bed, and then stick the iPod under some branches on the side of the pool. I look at the pile of dirt, the water, the sticks, and nod.

"I'm not sure yet if they'll do what I think. We have to wait till tomorrow to see if it works."

Aaron eyes the setup and nods too. I see his engineer brain working. "I think you're right!"

The boy has always been clever.

After we pack up to leave, I peek in to see if the kits are settled. They're already asleep next to the teddy bear. Despite their fight, the brothers are pressed together, their little arms wrapped snug, holding each other close.

# 18

THE NEXT DAY AARON, JACK, AND I OPEN
the clubhouse door and peer inside.

I feel a little thrill, even though I'd already seen it
this morning when I gave the kits their breakfast.

"That's a thing of beauty," I say, proudly, as if I'd
done it myself.

"That's a big mess," Jack says.

"It's *exactly* where you wanted them to do it, Madi,"
Aaron says, his eyes shining with wonder.

We gaze at the interlaced pile of sticks and mud.
Branches jab out of the mound at odd angles, looking
like a sad melty snowman. It leans precariously to one
side. Most of the material we'd brought in has been
used to make it.

The best part is *where* the kits built it. Along the side of the pool. Right on top of where I'd hidden the iPod.

The kits return our stare until Cooler seems to shrug and goes back to work. Grunting, he shoves a large stick into the door of their house. Phrag mutters a protest.

"It's obvious once you think about it," Aaron says. "Everyone knows beavers are the world's smelliest engineers."

"Step two of the plan worked," I say. "And they aren't smelly."

"What worked?" Jack says. "I don't know what's going on. All I see is a gigantic pile of mud in the middle of our clubhouse. Is that supposed to be a dam? That's the worst dam I've ever seen."

"I'll admit, they need practice." I worry again that they don't have anyone to teach them how to do these things with their parents gone.

"Why build one here?" Jack says. "It's in the way."

"The kits built where Madi wanted them to," Aaron explains. "She's using their instincts with the sound of running water to direct them."

"Ah," Jack says. But he still looks confused.

I'm not entirely clear myself about what to do next. "But I don't know if I can do it in the wild with other beavers. I'll need your help, Aaron."

"Well, that's never good. The last time you said that, I got attacked by a raccoon." Aaron loves to bring up the tree incident.

"He was just saying hello." I wave a hand. "Before we do anything, though, we should give Phrag and Cooler some kind of reward for all their work."

Even though beavers are nocturnal and don't care for bright sunshine, the small clubhouse isn't the right place for growing kits. They should be outside, somewhere they can play and learn how to swim and be beavers.

"Let's take them for a real swim," I say.

Mom's gone to work, so the only thing we need to worry about are predators and other beavers. As Aaron and I carry the kits toward the lake, I think about what I'd read in my beaver research. Beavers are fiercely protective of their territory and could attack other beavers they don't know. An adult beaver might kill one of the kits. Or they might decide the kits aren't a threat since they're so small. But there's no way to know, so we have to be cautious.

Aaron and I place the kits on the beach sand. They've already grown heavier since I rescued them. Must be all the sweet potatoes they've been eating. I was so relieved when I figured out they were old enough to eat solid food.

They huddle together and blink, not quite sure what to do.

Jack shucks off his shirt and grabs the boogie board from our box of beach toys.

"Banzaiiiii!" He runs screaming into the lake the way he always does.

Aaron enters the water in his usual method, tiptoeing inch by painful inch, flailing his arms. He's dramatically silent. The lake here isn't as sun-warmed as the channel, but at least it's not infested with leeches.

I carry the kits out on a bright pink flutter board. They float on the board and peer down at the water. Gaping owlishly at the lake and all the space around them, they seem to quiver with glee.

Cooler jumps off first. Once he sees his brother do

it, Phrag follows. They float on the surface, motionless. Little brown balls of fur shaped like torpedoes pointing right at me.

I drape myself over the board and float on my belly. Phrag scrapes me with his thrashing nails, trying to climb on my back.

"The thing I can't figure out now is how to make it work," I say to Aaron.

He floats next to me on a giant inflatable pineapple.

"They'll respond to the sound of running water," I say. "But we—Yowch!"

Cooler marches up the back of my leg. He hovers on my butt, looking down at Phrag victoriously.

"But we can't hide an iPod everywhere we want them to build," I continue. "And how do we know where to get the beavers to build, anyway?"

I watch Aaron's mind considering the problem as he bobs. He gets a particular blank look on his face when he's thinking hard.

"Maybe we can use the current somehow."

Phrag manages to haul himself up my right shoulder, clinging with nails as sharp as fork tines. He keeps up a running commentary: *Whee, whee, whee.* My back's going to be covered in red scratches by the end of our swim.

"What are you guys even talking about?" Jack complains. "How is that going to help the flooding? And it's not getting us any closer to solving the poaching case. If we find the shooter, we stop the beaver killings. Isn't that the important part? We need to investigate Mr. Archer."

Lid dog-paddles past me, biting the water as he splashes.

Jack has a point. I'm not even sure I know what I'm doing with the water experiment. Maybe we should follow his lead.

I dive under, dislodging the kits, then come up again. They voice their protests loudly. *Meee, meeeeee, meee.* They swim in circles around me while the dog swims in circles around Jack.

"Okay," I say. "Let's go see Mr. Archer." We have to catch the shooter before any more murders happen.

# 19

HOLLY ARCHER'S AN OLDER GIRL AT OUR school, going into eighth grade.

She lives in a small house on Birch Street, but she's not home when we knock on the door. No one is except some small dog inside who's freaking out about us being on the porch. Lid cocks his head at the door and whines.

"Well, we tried," Aaron says. "Let's go."

A truck pulls into the driveway. Mr. Archer steps out wearing work boots and a safety vest. "Hello, kids. You selling something?"

I wonder how Jack's going to get him to confess to shooting beavers.

"Did you shoot a beaver in Birch Creek a couple nights ago?" Jack blurts out.

I guess that's one way to go about it.

Jack's got his notebook out with a pen hovering over it like some kind of reporter. But his professional air is ruined by the crisscrossed red scratches on his arms from the raspberry bush, and his long dark hair plastered to one side of his face from our swim.

Mr. Archer stares at us and blinks. "Eh?"

"You bought shotgun shells, and a beaver showed up dead near your house." Jack's using his adult voice again. I'm almost impressed.

"A beaver? Shotgun shells . . . ?" Mr. Archer pauses to collect his thoughts, grabbing a metal lunch box and a big tube of paper off the front seat. He shuts the truck door and turns back to Jack. "Now, why would I want to shoot a beaver? Don't have the time to shoot anything. I think you're talking about the skeet ammo I got for Holly's birthday."

He stalks toward us on the trampled grass. "But if Holly told you about that, then you'd know she's practicing for the skeet competition. Gotta say, I'm perplexed. What are you kids up to?"

Aaron, who hates all confrontation but especially

with adults, starts slinking back toward the road. He aims a glare at me as if this is my fault.

"Sorry to bug you, Mr. Archer," I say. "We're just doing dares. We'll be going now." I grab Jack's sleeve and yank him.

Jack grudgingly follows as Aaron and I hightail it out of there. I glance behind me to see Mr. Archer still watching us, shaking his head.

Once we're around the corner, we slow down. I turn to Jack. "Did you know Holly does skeet shooting competitions?"

"Have to look into it. I'm not sure I buy it," Jack mumbles. His face is set with frustration. He suddenly seems unsure of himself.

"Mr. Archer better not tell my parents about this," Aaron says. "Next time, leave me out—" He stops short as we all take in the scene before us.

Hot fury spikes inside me, blinding and intense.

Two boys are playing with a baby animal in the ditch. They're tossing it back and forth.

"Stop that!" I charge toward them.

They drop the animal. I see them size up the three of us coming at them—or more likely, they see Jack

—then they grab their bikes and take off. The unlucky animal just lies there unmoving. My heart stutters, and when I get closer, it almost stops. It's a beaver kit.

For one silent, sickening moment, no one says anything.

I feel Aaron and Jack look to me.

"This is what happens when adult beavers get shot!" I shout.

Beavers don't wander around by themselves away from their lodge. If this kit's parents were still alive, they'd be protecting it.

My chest feels as though it's been carved out. I can barely bring myself to inspect the kit lying in the ditch.

When I carefully pick it up, my breath returns.

*It's alive.*

In fact, I can't see any injuries. The kit blinks at me in a daze.

Quickly I pull my shirt out and cradle the kit inside, next to my bare skin. It's smaller than Phrag and Cooler, and scrawny for a beaver. As if it's been starved.

"Hello, Xena," I say softly.

Aaron looks at me quizzically.

"Kits have sensitive eyes," I explain, thinking he's curious about why I covered the beaver. "The sunlight's too bright for her."

"How do you know it's female?" Jack asks.

"I don't. But she's a survivor. Doesn't she look like a warrior? Plus, I guessed that Phrag and Cooler were male, so I should change it up."

I peer into my shirt at the kit. She's strangely quiet, not like my other two at home. And she doesn't look nearly as sweet. In fact, I'd say she's glaring at me.

A choked groan escapes me as I recall beavers usually have more than one kit. "What happened to the rest of your family?"

Xena starts to quake. I clutch her protectively. I have to get her home, warm and dry, or she won't be a survivor after all.

# 20

THE NEXT DAY, XENA'S DOING A LOT better.

When we'd arrived home, I put her in isolation in her own box in the far corner of the clubhouse. If she was sick, I didn't want her giving anything to Phrag and Cooler. Nana had called it the "settle period"—when an animal needed to be kept warm and quiet when it first came to her.

Now I need to introduce them, because I don't have time to do everything twice. Between getting fresh lily roots, harvesting wild strawberries, changing their water a couple times a day, cleaning their bedding, cutting sweet potatoes, pilfering the fridge for fresh herbs, fruit, and yogurt, I've barely managed to show up for meals on time. My daily observations have been put on hold.

I plunk Xena on the floor next to the pool. Phrag and Cooler are perched on the boardwalk peeling twigs, but stop immediately. The three of them sniff the air.

The new kit takes the lead by waddling over and grabbing Cooler's face. Cooler isn't sure what to make of this small beaver with grabby hands. I think he's used to being the pushy one.

Xena stares at him, then smooths his cheeks, smells him, sucks on his ears. Cooler mutters uncertainly. Xena lets go of him and does the same to Phrag, inspecting him by running her fingers over his face. Phrag seems to enjoy the attention. *Meeee, meeeee, meeeee,* he says.

I'm pleased when Xena answers. She starts telling a long story. I imagine it's about her adventures wandering around alone looking for her parents. Cooler joins the discussion. He babbles his own tale, probably telling her how I braved the leeches and rescued them.

Fiercely, Xena grips Phrag with her short arms. Cooler objects at first, but then allows her to hug him, too. Xena seems thankful to not be alone anymore.

I'm glad she's more interested in them than in me. She hasn't really stopped glaring at me since she came, even after I fed her. That's a good thing for rehabilitating her back to the wild.

I watch Phrag and Xena cling to each other, mumbling to themselves. They're bonding and they aren't even from the same lodge. My observations today are happening right here. I pick up my logbook and write: *You don't need to be blood to be a family.*

I'm on my paddleboard, the kits following me along the shoreline. The board is rough under my toes as I balance to pull my paddle through the water. I glide silently along the surface. The kits are silent too — the only sounds are waves gently lapping along the rocky shore and birds in the trees. The kits take turns hopping on and off my board for short rides. It's thrilling to be out with the beavers like this, in their element. Was this how Jane Goodall felt when she was accepted by a family of wild chimps?

We're in the bay near the marsh when a tail slap shatters the calm. There's another beaver somewhere deep in the marsh. Unease grips me as I recall what adult beavers do to unfamiliar kits.

"Come on, guys—let's get out of here!" I try to turn the kits back home, but Xena has heard the splash too. She wants to investigate and she isn't used to listening to me like the other two. Worse, Phrag and Cooler follow her.

"No! Come back!" I rush after the kits, paddling hard.

There's an old wire fence lurking just under the surface at the entrance to the marsh. The kits swim through it with ease. Chasing after them, I'm stopped short when my board gets caught. I have to shove the top of the fence down with the paddle so I can skim over top. That takes a few seconds. When I look up again, the kits are gone.

"Phrag! Cooler!" I shout in panic. Where is that adult beaver? I can't let it kill them!

"Xena! Where are you guys?"

Suddenly a little brown head pops up next to me. Cooler eyes me with a mischievous twinkle, pleased with himself. Phrag and Xena appear beside him.

"Oh," I breathe in relief, turning the board around.

"You guys don't know how dangerous this is. We have to stay away from those wild beavers! Let's go home."

Cooler takes the lead. All three kits swim through the fence again. I try to follow, but this time my board gets even more stuck. The fin underneath is caught on the wire.

I have to get off the board to pry at it. The water is murky and as warm as bathwater. I'm frantic to get out of here. *Where is that wild beaver?*

My feet grip the wire like a tree frog's as I hang off it. The fence squeaks in protest at my weight. It's not letting go of the fin. Jiggling the board, I search around for the kits. They'd all kept going home and left me.

Just as I think this, Cooler appears, probably wondering what's taking me so long. He swims closer and watches me try to yank the paddleboard over the fence. I see him study the situation as though trying to figure it out. Then he's beside me, reaching for my board. He clasps the top of it and helps me pull it. When that doesn't work, Cooler glides to the wire and starts chewing it.

"No, Cooler. You'll hurt your teeth on that!" I push him away.

The determined kit sees that I'm still stuck. He swims underneath me and then surfaces behind the board. This time he pushes the board toward me.

Between the two of us, the board finally floats free and I hop back on. Cooler takes the lead again and I follow him toward home. The other two kits were waiting for us and Cooler rounds them up on the way.

As I paddle, I marvel how Cooler recognized that I was having a problem and came back to assist. He cared about what was happening to me! And I've always thought he was so grouchy toward me.

The most amazing part was that after he saw what the problem was, Cooler came up with three separate solutions to try to solve it.

I wish that the landowners could've seen him. No one would believe what Cooler just did. No one will listen when I tell them how smart beavers are.

Somehow, I have to show them.

A sudden tail slap restores my focus. Not far behind me now are two wild adult beavers. One is a medium size, the other large. Two sets of mean black eyes stare at me.

"Go away!" I yell.

They follow, drifting ominously closer, intent on the vulnerable kits in front of me.

Just in time, we arrive at our beach. I lunge off the board, anxiously scanning behind me.

"Come on, guys." I urge the kits out of the water. "We made it home."

That's when I hear Mom's car pull into the driveway. My blood freezes. She's way early.

The kits waddle with beaver speed across the beach. I can't carry them all. I can't hide them. I'm not even wearing a shirt over my bathing suit.

Glancing at the distance to the clubhouse, I calculate roughly that there's a greater chance of beavers growing wings than of us making it there in time.

I pick up Xena and start herding the others toward the shed. "Come on, hurry, faster . . . faster!" I hiss at them.

*Mmmmm, mmmm, mmmm*, they say.

I hear a car door slam. "Madi? Marley?"

I tickle Cooler's waggling tail to encourage him, and he curses at me. We're totally in the open, waltzing along the lawn as if we're going to a picnic. Mom only needs to glance around the corner of the house and my whole life will be ruined.

"I'm home!" The echo of Mom's voice tells me she's in the garage.

We're twenty feet from the clubhouse.

I've been lucky until now, I realize. I've gotten too comfortable, not careful enough. Is this the day I get caught?

Twelve feet.

The kits are moving as fast as they can, huffing and complaining the whole way like children at a park wanting to be picked up.

"Where is everyone?" Mom sounds so close that if the kits talk any louder, we're busted.

Eight feet.

Footsteps crunching, getting closer. She's coming round the corner. My heart smashes against my ribs.

Five feet.

I dive to the clubhouse door, open it wide, and toss Xena inside just as Mom appears. The door blocks the sight of Cooler collapsing in a heap of sulk, refusing to move any further. Phrag ambles cheerfully around his brother, his tail trailing sand.

"Oh, there you are!" Mom says.

My hands shaking, I pretend I'm just coming out of the clubhouse. Nudging Cooler with my toe, I shut the door behind me.

# 21

AFTER SPENDING THE REQUIRED AMOUNT of time with Mom before she left for Boston, I'm on fire with the need to get back to my plan to save *all* the beavers.

When Aaron and Jack meet me at Birch Creek, we stand on the bank and watch Lid chase frogs. My gaze travels from Lid to the culvert behind him, and I wish that I knew exactly *how* my plan will work.

It's a good sign that the large metal culvert, which looks like a tunnel underneath Birch Street, isn't clogged up with sticks anymore. That's what made the river back up and flood the road. To keep the beavers from damming it again, I need to think like a beaver.

I study the creek. Water ripples merrily over

rocks. The sun's hidden behind low-hanging clouds. There's a dense weightiness in the air that feels like expectation.

"The trickling-water sounds from the iPod in the clubhouse got the kits to make the dam," I say, thinking out loud. "We need to stop the beavers that live here from making a dam in there," I point to the culvert, "and put a dam where we want, like we did with the iPod."

I think of the way I'd pulled apart the dam downstream. Those beavers came to the sound.

Lid pounces along the muddy bank and midge flies scatter to zoom along the surface of the creek.

"What do *you* think?" I ask Aaron.

Aaron picks up a stick and holds it in the current, stretching out to protect his shoes. The water gurgles its way around the stick. I watch Aaron inspecting the area, biting his lip with a blank expression, thinking hard.

"We need fat poles," he says. "To put them here and here." He points in the current upstream of the culvert.

"Poles like these?" Jack says. He's above us, crouched on a ledge of dirt near the trail that the snowmobiles use in winter. A rock the size of a truck has shifted and split away from the trail, creating a long, deep crevice in the ground. Jack points into the crevice.

Aaron and I scrabble up the embankment of loose rocks to see what he's pointing at. The crevice is narrow and smells like freshly turned earth. Lying at the bottom on bedrock are three steel poles. They look like old highway signs.

"They must've fallen down there," Jack says.

I kneel on the edge of the dirt and stretch my arm down, but I can't reach the poles. And I don't think I can wedge in next to the rock.

Jack and I look at Aaron.

Aaron's face falls in dismay. "*Come* on! I always do it!"

I look at the unsturdy tree clinging to the shallow dirt next to the crevice. If Jack holds on to the tree, we can form a human chain and Aaron can lower himself to retrieve the poles.

"Do you trust me?" I ask.

"What kind of question is that?" Aaron says. "Of course I don't trust you. And I'm not that small!"

But soon we're stretched out from the tree with

me in the middle and Aaron on his belly, hanging into the crevice. He clings to my hand and reaches with his other. The spindly tree, which might actually be dead if I'm being honest, bends under our combined weight.

"What if we lowered you by your feet?" I suggest.

"No feet!" Aaron grunts, his voice muffled by the crevice. "Just an inch more. I nearly got 'em."

"If this branch breaks . . ." Jack says, but doesn't finish the thought.

The tree lets out a threatening creak.

Aaron's head pops up with the sound. "Retreat!" he yells.

I pull Aaron back, frustrated. "Wish we had a rope."

"Oh. Uh, could we use this?" Jack reveals that he's wearing Lid's leash around his middle as a belt.

"Only if your pants don't fall down," I say.

"What?" Jack grips the leash as though reconsidering.

"What's wrong, Jack?" Aaron crows. "Don't want us seeing your Cookie Monster underwear?"

Jack will never live down the underwear incident when we were nine.

"Would you two focus!" I snatch the leash.

This time Aaron goes back into the crevice hanging on to the handle of the leash with me on the other end. He reaches the bottom and hands the poles up to us. One has a small metal triangle attached to the pole. It's a snowmobile sign.

"This is perfect," Aaron says. "It'll cause more resistance in the water and create turbulence."

Jack nods as if he knows exactly what turbulence is.

The next challenge is getting the poles stuck far enough into the riverbed so they stay upright. Standing up to his thighs in flowing river water, Aaron has given up on his shoes staying dry.

We hammer the tops of the poles with rocks. Aaron has chosen the narrowest part of the creek to sink the line of poles across. Jack does his own pole, most of Aaron's, then helps me with mine. I have to admit his solid build's handy to have around sometimes.

Once the pounding and ringing stop, we listen to the sound of the water rushing around the poles. It gurgles and gushes, hopefully sounding like water going down the drain of a bathtub.

By the time we're done, we're all waterlogged rats

covered in sweat and scratches from the rocks. Jack blows mud out of his nose.

The sky clears with an optimism I don't quite share. My wet clothes feel steamy under the sun. We squeak as we climb back onto the muddy bank.

"Now we wait," I say. The experiment had been a success in the clubhouse with the kits, but surveying our effort out here, I wonder why I ever thought this would work. And thinking of the kits in the clubhouse, I'm suddenly anxious about how long we've been gone.

"Let's go feed the kits," I say.

"My shoes are squishy," Aaron complains, as we clomp back to the ATV.

# 22

IT ISN'T UNTIL WE PULL INTO THE DRIVE-
way that I remember it's Friday.

My yard is full of people standing around laughing.
Some are hauling coolers out of the back of trucks, and
some are on the lawn doing yoga poses. Teenagers are
so weird.

"What's all this?" Aaron says, looking around with
concern.

"I forgot about Marley's party."

We hop off the ATV in the driveway and stow our
helmets. Lid flops on a cool spot on the cement floor
of the garage. Music thumps from somewhere — I can't
see the source.

"It doesn't matter," I say. "Let's go feed the kits."

We weave through a group of people carrying

benches to the fire pit in the backyard. A girl loses her flip-flop and falls to the ground, laughing with a high-pitched squeal. I want to tell her she doesn't have to be so loud. Everyone's already looking at her.

Marley's best friends, Brenda and Pam, are sitting on the patio playing guitar. Trevor walks by and gives me a little salute. I recognize him even though it's been almost two years since my sister had gone out with him on her first date. I don't recognize everyone though, there are so many. And some of them look older. I wonder if Marley even knows them.

My sister intercepts us. She's with Cal, wearing his straw cowboy hat and cutoff jean shorts that show off her long legs.

"What are you turdlets doing here?" She points at Aaron and Jack.

"Nothing!" they both say in unison.

"Relax," Cal says, draping an arm over Marley's shoulders. He takes a swig out of a Pepsi can. "Let the little dudes stay. What are they hurting?"

I adjust my opinion about Cal. He's *way* better than any of Marley's old boyfriends.

"Don't. Talk. To anyone," Marley warns us.

Jack, Aaron, and I exchange a look. We turn as one and skulk off in the other direction, out of Marley's line of sight.

As we head toward the clubhouse, the smell of smoke catches my attention. Someone's started a fire in the pit. There's a pile of wood next to it, and an ax leans against the pile.

I take another look. The ax head is green. Something about that makes me pause. Where have I seen a bright green ax before?

Brushing my hair out of my eyes, I briefly search my memory.

"That's the ax!" Jack hisses. He grabs me and Aaron. His fingers squeeze my arm.

"What ax?" Aaron asks.

"Remember Mr. Kang's trees? How they had paint marks? That must be the ax used to cut them down."

"Hmm," Aaron says, not convinced.

"How many axes do you think have been painted lime green?" Jack says, full of renewed enthusiasm. "This is the lead we've been looking for. Why didn't I think of the green on the trees? The poacher could be right here at this party." He gazes around suspiciously.

"I don't think that's going to . . ." I start to say. But then someone next to the fire picks up the ax.

"Maybe it's his!" Jack steps forward.

Just as I think that Jack could be right, I notice something much worse. I clap a hand over my mouth. All thoughts of catching a poacher vanish.

"Oh no!" I say, and take off running.

The boys race behind me. We arrive at the club-house at the same time, piling on top of each other as we brake. The door is wide open. *Someone's been in here and left the door open.*

I rush in, scanning around in a panic. "Phrag! Cooler! Are you here? Xena?"

I drop to my knees in front of their cardboard house and peer in. No sign of them. I lift the box, shake it. Nothing inside. My blood turns to ice. I sit down hard.

*The kits are gone.*

# 23

WHEN I WAS SEVEN, MARLEY AND I went on an adventure.

She was trying to show me a baby deer she'd heard about by the ball diamonds. Marley knew I'd want to see it, so she drove me on the ATV. She was old enough to take it out, but she wasn't as familiar with the trails as I am now. We got lost on the way.

Marley was afraid of going down a strange trail and getting stuck, so we left the ATV and tried walking back the way we'd come. That just got us more turned around.

I remember her crying—that's what scared me the most. She was my big sister and wasn't supposed to be afraid of anything.

"It's okay, Marley," I said. I wished I'd paid more attention to where we were going. I felt I'd let her down.

She was sitting on the ground with her face buried in her hands. I reached out and patted her head like she was a spooked animal. My sister pulled me down on her lap, hugged me tight.

She kept saying, "I'm sorry, Mads. I'm supposed to protect you, but I always screw up."

We sat there awhile, just holding on to each other, and somehow it made us both feel better. We stood, brushed the dirt off, and walked home as if we'd known all along where we were going. Later, Dad went and got the ATV. We never told them what happened, only that the ATV stalled so we'd walked the rest of the way.

That feeling of being lost and scared floods through me again as I stare at the empty cardboard box. Is that how the kits feel right now? The three of them are out there alone somewhere. I hate to imagine them huddling together, lost and vulnerable.

"No, no, no!" I say, feeling dizzy. "We've got to find them!"

I shove Aaron and Jack and we tumble outside.

Standing there a moment, we survey the party that's going on as though nothing awful has happened. Jack and Aaron look just as worried as me.

"If I was a scared beaver kit, where would I go?" Aaron asks me.

Right. I'm the expert. Calm down and think.

"The beach?" I suggest. "When we go there, it's fun. They'll remember it."

We dash toward the lake. A few of Marley's friends lounge on our small beach, chatting. Gentle waves lap at the shore. No beaver-shaped torpedoes in sight. We sprint up to the girls, accidently kicking sand on their towels.

"Hey!"

"Have you seen any beavers around here?" Jack asks.

They look up at us and laugh. "Beavers? Well, let me think. What did they look like?"

Aaron starts indicating with his hands about the size of the kits, but I grab his arm and pull him away.

"Never mind," I say. To Aaron I whisper, "They wouldn't laugh if they'd seen them."

Where else could they be? Is Xena terrified of all

the people around, remembering the last time she was out in the world? I wonder if the two brothers will gain strength from each other out here like my sister and I did. Are they feeling brave because they're together? I hope so.

"We have to find them. Before anything bad happens." I look out across the water. What if the beaver family came and killed them? What if they've fallen somewhere and got stuck or hurt and can't get out? A terrifying thought suddenly occurs, and I spin toward the driveway.

"Come on!" I race ahead. As we run, I shout, "They wouldn't have gone out on the road, right?"

Jack pales but doesn't answer.

Why do we live so close to the road? No one will see the little fur balls waddling along until it's too late. And Mrs. Stinton always drives crazy.

I should've been more careful. I knew this party was happening. How did I not recognize that they'd be in danger? I shouldn't have left them alone so long. I should've been here protecting them.

We leap over a pile of blankets someone's dumped

on the edge of our driveway. Aaron doesn't quite clear them.

I hear his soft "Oof!" behind me but don't wait.

Jack and I sprint down the driveway toward the gate. Which I've never thought to notice before, since it's always open. Really, why even have a gate then? Can't it be closed just this once?

We reach the gate and pause, catching our breath. I'm suddenly terrified of what we'll find. What if they did get hit by a car?

All three of them.

I can't look out at the road. But I have to.

# 24

I INCH TOWARD HAWK LAKE ROAD AND
search up and down the length of it.

No vehicles. No little brown bodies anywhere. Jack
and I both sigh in relief.

Aaron arrives, winded. "Wish we could track them
somehow," he wheezes.

Jack slaps his own forehead. "Right. C'mon."

We follow Jack to the garage where we'd left Lid.

"Let's go track the beavers!" Jack says to him.

The dog, who'd been out cold, lifts his head and
gives us a look, which I easily translate.

"Yes, right now," I tell him.

"We have to start at the clubhouse," Jack explains.
"He follows a scent in the direction it moves, toward
where the smell is newest."

At least it sounds like Jack knows what he's doing. He points to the empty cardboard box. "Find them, Lid. Where'd they go?"

Lid sticks his nose to the ground and starts snuffling. I feel hopeful. He continues out to the lawn, and then beelines for the house. We dash after him, careful to avoid bumping into loitering teenagers.

The side door is propped open with so many people coming and going, so we chase him inside.

"This doesn't feel right," I say. "Are we sure he knows what he's doing?"

"Of course," Jack says. "He's a trained tracker."

We find him in the kitchen. Someone has spilled a bag of Cheezies and Lid's busy hoovering the floor. He lifts his head briefly to acknowledge us, his black snout coated in bright orange crumbs.

"Not helpful, Lid!" Aaron says.

Jack looks deflated.

I turn away, frustration making me want to scream. "Let's go back outside. That dog was only following his stomach again. We're wasting time!"

A desperate fear is mounting inside me. *We have to find them.*

"Let's split up," I say. "Aaron, you check under the back deck. Jack, try the hedges. I'll look around the garage."

We break off and I run around the corner of the house. I crash into Cal.

"Hey. Slow down. What's wrong?"

"I'm . . . looking for a baby beaver," I say. I don't have time to explain it. But Cal hardly blinks. He just nods, looking serious.

"Don't worry, I'll help you find your toy. Where did you last see it?"

"Not a toy. They were in the shed. Do you know if anyone went into the shed?"

"No, sorry, I didn't notice. But it's okay, we'll search. Right after I get back. I was just about to get more ice." He jingles the keys in his hand.

That's when I notice what he has in his other hand. A bright green ax.

I gape at him as he stashes it in the back of his pickup. Maybe Jack's wrong. Maybe there are lots of green axes.

Cal winks at me as he hops in his truck and drives off.

My mind plays back the conversation where my parents had asked if Cal had a summer job and Marley said he worked on his dad's farm. His dad's a *farmer*. Could Cal be the killer? All this time, the killer has been dating my sister? But he's so *nice*.

My knees feel like gummies as I start toward the hedgerows on the side of the house. I have to find Jack and tell him.

The sound of a vehicle pulling up behind me makes me stop again. Is that Cal back already? I whirl around . . . and freeze.

Mom steps out of her car. Her eyes bug out as she takes in all the people on her lawn. And then they land on me.

# 25

"WHAT IN HEAVEN . . . ?"

"Uh, Mom. Hi. I thought you were in Boston?"

She slams the car door. "My flight was canceled."

I watch as she absorbs the music, the laughter, the bonfire, the coolers, the blankets, and the yoga poses.

"Where is she?"

"It's not what it looks like," I begin. Lame. Of course, it's exactly what it looks like, but it feels like something I'm supposed to say.

Marley chooses that moment to come around the corner. "Cal, are you back so—?" She stops dead, her mouth hanging open.

"Yes, it seems I've surprised you," Mom says.

The hedges beside Marley start shaking. Mom gasps and covers her heart.

Marley doesn't even flinch as Jack crawls out. He stands, twigs sticking out of his hair, and gapes at us. Then he turns to crawl right back in.

"Oh, no, Jack," Mom says, recovering quickly. "You come with me."

"Yes, ma'am." Jack spears me with accusing eyes as if this is my fault. Why does everyone blame me? He brushes past toward the car.

"I'm sure Aaron is around here somewhere," Mom says. "I'll take the boys home. When I get back, I expect all of this," she spins her hand in the air, "to have vanished. And then we will have a long chat about responsibility."

Once Mom leaves with Jack and Lid and Aaron, Marley starts hollering for everyone to go home. There's a lot of complaining, but Marley can be a scary force when she wants to be. In short order everyone's packed up, stuffed in their vehicles, and gone. Then it's just me and my sister left to clean up.

"Marley," I say, "the kits are missing."

"Not my problem." She tosses a stack of blankets into the garage.

I grab an empty cooler and slide it out of the way. "I have to tell you something."

"Not now."

"I think Cal's the one who shot the kits' parents."

"What?" Marley stops her frantic cleaning long enough to look at me. "What are you talking about?"

I count on my fingers. "Someone was over by the channel and shot two beavers. Then they went to Mr. Kang's house and cut down his trees with an ax that'd been painted green. They tried to make it look like a beaver did it! Maybe to frame Mr. Kang for shooting the beavers, I don't know."

Marley makes an impatient noise and picks up an empty garbage bag. "You've been hanging around Jack too long. How do you even know the person went from the channel to Mr. Kang's? And I don't see the connection to Cal." She stomps a can on the ground and pitches it in the bag.

"The connection is Cal's dad is a farmer. He's a landowner who hates beavers, so there's motive. And he has a green ax. Lid did a track! He found the shotgun shells

—Jack has them. And he found butts, though he ate those." I pause. "Does Cal smoke?"

Marley snorts. "No, he doesn't smoke. See? Before you go . . . accusing . . ." She trails off and gets a strange look on her face.

"What?" I demand.

She shakes her head and stomps a can.

I growl in frustration. This conversation is pointless anyway. "The worst news is the kits are missing. Someone from your stupid party let them out so you have to help me find them!"

"Are you serious? That's the worst news? Hello, did you not notice *Mom?* She's coming back any minute. What do you think will happen if we haven't cleaned up?"

She's right of course. A heavy silence settles over us as we pitch garbage and mull over our own personal nightmares. By the time Mom comes home, I'm anxious to just get it over with.

She orders us into the kitchen, where we sit at the table. I ignore something sticky on the floor by my foot. Mom unwraps her scarf and sets it on the placemat in front of her. She folds it in half and then in half again, smoothing it out carefully.

"I see that some things need to be fixed around here," she begins. "Starting with you, young lady." She points to Marley.

My sister makes a face and crosses her arms over her chest.

"We've let you have too much freedom. I see that now. Too much free time and not enough responsibilities. Well, that's going to change right now. You're getting a job."

"*What?*" Marley slams her hands on the table. "But I have one. I look after Madi."

"Not anymore. You're going to start working at the feed store. They're looking for summer help. It will all be arranged."

"The *feed store?*" Marley moans. She covers her face and then crumples dramatically into a heap on the table.

"I can't understand why you don't take more of an interest in things, Marley. Why can't you be more like . . . other people? You should want to work toward something other than boys. You need goals. You need to find a hobby, something that you love to do."

"We can't all be perfect like *other people*."

"You need more commitment in your life. If not, then you'll work to productively fill all the time on your hands."

"Can I be excused?" I say. I've got the uneasy feeling they're talking about me, and for the first time, I wish I weren't included. Plus, I need to keep searching for the kits.

"No, you may not. I'm not finished. I hold both of you responsible for taking care of the house while your father and I can't. We're all in this together as a family."

"Hah!" Marley screams. "You're one to talk about family. When does Madi ever get to see you? She's growing up like an orphan. Dad's gone half the time. And you're always gone in the morning and come home late at night. All you *do* is work. Nice commitment to the stuff that matters, Mom."

Mom goes still. The color drains from her face as if she's been slapped. Marley also looks as though she's in shock. For some annoying reason, when Marley's rattled, I am too. I feel as if I've just been hit by a bus.

The room goes very quiet.

The fridge hums to life.

Slowly, Mom rises from her chair. "You have a point," she says quietly. "Excuse me, I need a minute. I'll be right back."

Mom walks down the hall with precise steps. *Click, click, click.*

Marley and I stay seated across from each other. Her face is pale with twin blotches of pink high on her cheeks. When our eyes meet, something in her expression falls, like when a log is removed from a dam, compromising its strength.

For a moment I see a little of my old sister. The sister who used to help me do my hair like hers and jump on the tire tubes in the lake and eat popcorn upside down hanging off the couch. Back when even though we sometimes got lost, we always had each other.

Marley reaches out her hand. "I—"

A shriek from the bathroom cuts off whatever she wanted to say.

Marley and I race toward it. Mom leans against the bathroom door, gaping at something inside. When I get close enough, a fat ball of dread lodges in my guts even as I spin with relief. There are two beaver kits trying to climb out of our toilet.

They see me and raise their arms. *Uppy, uppy.*

# 26

"WHAT . . . HOW . . . WHERE . . . ?"

Mom's got a lot of questions.

The kits aren't happy about the situation either. They're taking turns standing on each other's heads trying to pull themselves out of the bowl. But since most of their weight is in their butts, their little arms are straining hard.

Mom draws a breath and starts again with a shriek. "What *are* those things?"

I'm too focused on rescuing the distressed kits to answer. The more important question is: *Where is Xena?*

And it's a mystery how Phrag and Cooler even got in the toilet. Did they come in on their own looking for me? Maybe they remembered their bath and yogurt dip in here. Did they fall in after investigating the sound of water? Or did someone from the party put them in here as a joke?

I hold them close to my chest to calm my pounding heart. Their crying calms too. They leave a wet spot on my shirt. Lid had tried to tell us the kits were in the house. Some animal whisperer I am.

"They're only harmless beaver kits, Mom. This one is Phragmites." I smooth his fur and he clutches my finger with one hand.

"He's the sensitive type," I continue. "He likes it when you breathe in his face. And this here's Cooler. He's got grabby hands, but his heart's in the right place."

Maybe if I act casual, Mom won't be mad about the kits.

"Madison Lewis."

*Uh-oh.*

"Why do we have a pair of beavers in the house? I thought I was pretty clear on the topic of strays."

"It's kind of a long story."

"Well, you will have a whole four days at home to tell me about it, because you certainly won't be in

Stratton next week." Her carefully calm voice tells me she's top-level mad.

She fixes me with her stony expression. "I guess you weren't as keen on seeing Jane Goodall as I thought."

"NO! Just . . . wait. I need to go!" This isn't happening. I brace myself against the wall. "Please! I *have* to meet her!"

"If you wanted to go so badly, you should've thought of that before you brought those beavers home."

"But they would've *died!*" I take a shaky breath and then yell, "*If you see something, do something!*"

Mom lets out a pained sigh, pinching the bridge of her nose. "One cares too much, the other doesn't care enough." She opens her eyes. "Let's everyone just take a moment. Can you at least put them outside somewhere for now?"

I don't need to be told twice. Hurrying out of the bathroom with the kits, I stop only to grab some food. I place them on the kitchen counter while I rummage in the fridge. They might be trailing a little toilet water with their wet butts.

*"Madison!"*

"Right. Sorry. I'm going." I sweep them off the counter and out the side door.

Phrag and Cooler seem ecstatic to be back home after their grand adventure. They race around the clubhouse, inspecting everything.

I fill the food pan with French toast along with their favorite treats, and toss the last of the lily roots in their pool.

Mom's words sink in as I work.

I'm not going to meet Jane Goodall.

I'm not going to get to ask her my questions . . . questions I should've asked my own nana when I had the chance.

I sit on the floor before I fall. Phrag and Cooler are still tearing around the clubhouse. I watch them a little more closely. Their cries, which I thought were excitement, are actually different from any noises I've heard them make before. It's more of a keening wail.

"I've got your food in the pool," I point out.

They're so loud that Mom's going to hear from the house. Not that it matters anymore. What is she going to do now that she knows about these two? If the

Township takes them and releases them, they'll die. I have to try to make her see reason.

The kits continue their frantic movements. "You guys are freaking me out. Look, you don't even have to share with—" My stomach drops as I realize: *They're looking for Xena!*

Phrag crawls into my lap. He bumps my shirt with his nose before looking directly at me. He's asking where his adopted sister is.

I'm filled with a pulsing hot sorrow. How would I feel if I'd lost Marley? That day on the ATV, at least we were together. I don't know what I would've done if she hadn't come home.

I can't look at Phrag. The kits were all counting on me to keep them safe, and I failed them.

A broken sound escapes me as I cover my face. My world is imploding. I feel sick with regret knowing that I was responsible for these lives and now Xena is most likely dead.

*Mom was right.* I'm too young and I don't know what I'm doing.

It's bad that Mom found the kits. It's really bad that

I'm not allowed to go to Stratton and meet Jane Good-all. But far worse is that I've lost Xena when she was relying on me.

There's a knock on the clubhouse door and Mom comes in. I sit up. She wrinkles her nose while looking around, taking it all in. The pool, the potting soil, the sticks and the gardening supplies, the sagging cardboard box, and the distressed kits currently covered in mashed yams.

"I see," she says.

"You can't tell anyone, Mom," I begin. "Without Nana, Willow Grove doesn't have a wildlife rehabber. They'll take them away and won't know what to do with them."

She looks at me with a torn expression. "Madi, you know I have to turn them in. It's illegal to have the beavers here. You've put me in a bad position."

She spies the box I'd kept Xena in when I first brought her home. "Are these two the only animals you have?"

I open my mouth to tell her, but my throat squeezes so hard, I only squeak. What can I say to her to properly explain how amazing and smart and vulnerable these kits are? How can I find the right words to get her to understand?

I look toward Phrag and Cooler and see something that might help. I grab the logbook from the table and hand it to Mom.

"It's all in here."

# 27

## THE NEXT MORNING I'M READY.

Or at least I thought I was, until the people show up with dog crates and gloves and catch poles. I can't even watch as Phrag and Cooler are loaded into the van and carted away.

The worry over where they'll end up and if they'll be properly cared for clamps around my rib cage, crushing the breath out of me.

After the kits are gone, I smash around in the club-house, piling all Nana's old rehabber tools and equipment. I stack her logbooks. I box up all the formula and feed pans. The cotton balls and eyedroppers and bedding.

It takes most of the day. Once it's done, I look

around at the bare shelves and all the new space in the clubhouse. Now it just feels empty. My heart is as hollow as the bones of a bird.

My cell phone rings. I pull it out of my backpack.

"Hi, Mom," Aaron says. That's code to let me know he's borrowed an adult's phone again so he can "call home." I wish he had his own so we can text like normal people.

"Jack and I are at the bridge," he continues. "You'd better get down here."

*The bridge.* My experiment at Birch Creek.

A surge of frustration washes over me like a black wave. "I can't make it. I'm extremely grounded."

"You're missing Jack saying that I'm a brilliant engineer. I think I should get it in writing."

"Why?" I practically shout into the phone. "Did it work? Tell me what it looks like!"

"You've got to see it for yourself to appreciate it."

"Great," I say, and hang up. At one point, the experiment felt very important, but now it's impossible to summon the confidence I once had in it.

I make my way into the house, wander into the den

and perch on the sofa, turning on the TV. What do people *do* in the summer when they aren't caring for three busy kits, and saving a town's beaver population?

Marley comes in with her usual rhino stomp. She steals the remote before flopping next to me. "At least you won't smell like rat anymore."

"Really? That's all you've got to say? Xena is *gone* because of your friends. And the other kits are gone because of me. And they didn't smell. Not that you'd care to notice."

I get up to leave. Marley grabs my arm and flings me backwards onto the sofa. Throwing a cushion on my back, she sits all her weight on it and traps me like she used to do to keep me from eating the chips.

She balances on the cushion now, expecting me to fight. But I have no more fight left in me.

"What do you want?" My voice is muffled by the couch pressing into my face.

Marley sighs. "You're no fun anymore."

The pressure comes off as she removes the cushion and lets me up. "I just wanted to tell you to make sure you had your little nerdlings here tomorrow morning. Before nine. It's important."

"Uh, *grounded?*"

"Well, Mom's planning on going to the office in the morning, so she won't be here to ask. Figure it out."

Shortly before nine the next morning, I pull up to our dock with my mystified friends.

"But did she give you any clue?" Aaron asks.

"If you ask one more time, I'm going to dunk your shoes in the lake." I tie off the bow line on a cleat. "I only know Marley's starting work today at the feed store and Cal's picking her up."

"Perfect," Jack says, steadying himself on Lid before jumping out of the boat. "I have to interview Cal."

Since I told Jack the green ax was Cal's, he seems confident about solving the case. What I didn't tell Jack is that I hope he has it wrong. I don't want Cal to be the shooter. I don't want my sister dating a poacher. Then again, if Jack doesn't solve this case, we don't stop the shooter. More kits could be orphaned.

It all feels hopeless. Did I ever really think we could make a difference?

"Have you found Xena?" Aaron asks, which reopens the fissure inside me.

Both boys see my face and don't ask any more questions.

A cold ache settles around my heart. I search for something good to focus on or I'm going to bawl. "Dad's coming home tonight. We're getting a blueberry pie."

As we make our way to the house, Cal's truck pulls up. Without Cal. The driver hops out wearing a straw hat and plaid shirt. He looks like a slightly older version of Cal.

Marley meets us from the side door.

The driver asks her, "You ready? I'm in a hurry."

"'Sup, Dan." She gestures toward us. "This is my sister, Madi, and her friends, Jack and Aaron."

I stare at her, trying to recall the last time she'd referred to my friends by their actual names.

"This is Cal's *brother*, Dan," she says, giving me a pointed look. Then she turns to Dan. "I'm ready to go. You got a smoke?"

Dan looks as confused as the rest of us, but he automatically reaches into his shirt pocket. "I didn't know you smoked."

Marley shrugs, tucks the cigarette behind her ear, and jumps into the truck.

As Dan steps round to the driver's door, my thoughts race. Did my sister just set it up for us to meet Dan? Did she *help* us?

Jack is faster. He points. "I knew it! It's *your* ax! You shot the beavers!"

Dan pauses, looking startled. "What the—what? Who told you that?"

Jack's eyes go round, as though he can't believe Dan just confessed. Can't believe he was actually right. But he pulls it together in the next breath. "My detector dog tracked you. He found your shotgun shells and cigarette butts with your DNA all over them. The authorities are going to thank me."

Dan's starting to twitch. "I don't know what you kids think you saw, but nobody in this town's going to care about dead beavers." He wrenches the truck door open.

"Mr. Kang's going to care about his trees being cut," Jack says.

Dan's mouth hangs open as he stares.

"Were you trying to frame Mr. Kang for shooting

the beavers?" Aaron steps out from behind Jack long enough to ask. "That doesn't make any sense."

It bugs Jack when he can't figure something out.

Dan produces a series of snorts. He drops his keys, fumbles on the ground for them, hits his head on the side mirror coming up, then hustles into the seat, slamming the door.

"Beavers cut down Mr. Kang's trees!" he yells, as he peels away.

Dust from Dan's truck is still hanging in the air while the three of us stare at each other.

Jack pumps his fist and roars. "We got him! Lid, did you hear that? You did it!"

Lid wags his tail lazily and gives us a knowing, wide-mouthed grin. Then pauses when a yellow butterfly lands on his head.

"My first solved murder case," Jack says, smugly. "Come on, Madi. Let's go back to the Township office."

I'm starting to feel a fire grow in my belly. Something Dan just said is sinking in. *Nobody in this town's going to care about dead beavers.*

He's right. The whole town's gone beaver crazy. As

long as the flooding keeps happening, everyone will keep hating beavers.

I think of the bridge experiment. Grounded or not, I have to get over there. Someone needs to show the Township how to stop the flooding.

# 28

I STASH THE ATV IN THE USUAL SPOT IN the bushes, and we make our way to the Birch Street bridge.

Anxiously I recall when the road was blocked because it was underwater. I know the boys have seen our pole setup, but maybe they were mistaken? It's hard to believe the beavers did what I hoped. Did I truly get them to stop damming the culvert?

As we hurry along the forest trail, sunbeams shoot straight through the trees glowing in brilliant lines. They illuminate the pollen in the air, something you wouldn't know was there unless you were looking for it.

When we pop out onto the road, I see it is indeed still dry. Lid jogs ahead and we follow him down the embankment. I stop short. My breath escapes in a small "oh" as I take in the sight. It's magnificent.

*The experiment worked.*

Jack claps me on the shoulder. "They dammed our stakes instead of the culvert."

"Madi." Aaron prods me. "You can control wild beavers!"

We grin at each other. "I can control where beavers build," I repeat, cautiously.

I stare again at the muddy wall of sticks that's been built all along the stake line we'd placed so carefully. It's exactly what I hoped the beavers would do. It's exactly where Aaron had figured a dam could go without flooding the road. They left the culvert alone.

"Now can we go tell the Township?" Aaron asks.

"About the poacher, too!" Jack says.

I nod. "We're ready."

The Township office is five blocks away. We pound along the sidewalk, Lid loping beside us. Exhaust fumes from an old car rattling past make me wheeze. The heat from the pavement blasts us in waves. Even my knees are sweating. The boys whoop and shove each other, laughing as we run.

By the time we get there, we're buzzing with excitement. Bursting into the office, sweaty and babbling loudly about the dam, we see at once there's a different secretary today.

"Where's Carrie?" I ask.

"Vacation." The new lady looks as though she's caught a whiff of Lid after he eats hot dogs. But we left him outside this time.

She surveys us. "Can I help you?" Then she smiles with her mouth but frowns with her eyes, and everyone knows you can't trust a person who does that.

I try anyway. "You need to get an inspector to the bridge to take a look at what we've done."

"Yes, I'm sure." The lady adjusts the glasses on her nose. She turns back to her computer.

I draw on my renewed courage and insist. "Seriously, I think we fixed the beaver problem."

"We don't have a beaver problem." She peers at us over her glasses. "Where're your parents?"

"We need to see your supervisor!" Aaron yells,

slapping the counter. His unruly hair shudders as if in shock. Jack and I join the secretary in staring at him.

"I beg your pardon, young man!"

"You have to believe us," I say, trying to reel in the situation. "We directed the beavers to build a dam."

The way she flattens her lips makes my stomach sink. "So, you're saying you *made* the beavers make a dam?"

"She controls them!" Aaron explains pointing at me.

"Very funny. Now go outside to play. Go on." She points to the door, and then promptly ignores us as though we aren't still standing there.

"We're not finished," Jack says, flustered. "I solved the poaching problem, too. I have evidence—"

"We *do not* have a poaching problem!" The secretary uses a tone that stops Jack from finishing his big reveal.

"But . . ." Aaron trails off under the secretary's withering glare.

This is getting us nowhere. The three of us share a look. With long faces and shoulders sagging, we slink out to join Lid.

Wandering over to a bench, we sit in the shade of a tree to regroup. Aaron pulls his feet up and hugs his knobby knees. "Should've seen that coming. Adults are never going to listen to a bunch of kids trying to explain that we know who's been shooting beavers. That we *made* them not dam the culvert."

"This isn't fair!" Jack says. "She didn't even want to hear about the evidence."

A man walks by wearing the same kind of clothes the school janitor wears. "Hey, Jack," he says. Then he walks into the Township office.

Aaron and I both look at Jack. He jumps up, not meeting our eyes.

"Who's that?" Aaron asks.

"What? Oh, him. Just Mom's new friend. It's not important." There's a pause as Jack hurls rocks at a tree.

I see Aaron thinking. "Boyfriend?"

"No!" Alarmingly, Jack looks like he might cry.

I search for something to say to get past the weirdness that's descended on us. The last thing we need to deal with right now is Jack's family drama.

"Does he work for the Township?" Aaron presses.

Jack shrugs. "I guess."

"So, is he your confidential informant?" Aaron sounds pleased to have figured it out. Though, as usual, he's somehow oblivious to Jack's feelings.

"I don't actually talk to him. I just heard stuff he said to my mom. It doesn't matter anyway, since no one even cares that I've solved the case." Jack hurls another rock, which bounces off the tree and nails me in the shoulder.

"Ow!"

Instead of apologizing, Jack barks out a laugh, even though I can tell by the tightness in his face that he feels sorry. At least it makes him stop pelting the tree and come over to slump on the bench.

"We need a plan," I say, rubbing my shoulder. On either side of me, Jack and Aaron stay silent.

Lid's the only one who looks happy. He's found some used gum stuck under the bench. He sits beside us, chewing thoughtfully.

A determination has replaced my earlier hopelessness. We've come so far. I risked *everything* for this — it has to be worth it. We are not going to be stopped by a cranky secretary.

We need evidence, like Jack said. I need to take pictures of the poles we placed as proof. And we need to talk with someone who does care. Someone who was interested in me being an animal whisperer. But we can't wait till she gets back from vacation.

"Jack. Your mom's friend would know Carrie since he works with her. Maybe he knows where we can find her?"

I wait quietly while emotions play across Jack's features. His eyes narrow in anger, and then his lips press with stubbornness. His face pales with something like grief.

As I watch Jack, I realize that being an animal whisperer and studying the body language of animals has sort of helped me listen to people better too.

Jack sighs. "Fine. I'll talk to him. Wait here."

# 29

CARRIE STUDIES THE RIVER UNCERTAINLY.
"So what am I looking at?"

It hadn't been hard to find her once Jack got the address for us. And just as I'd hoped, the pictures we showed her on my phone made her curious enough to come to the culvert.

It takes a while, but we tell her all of it. About the day we'd discovered the adult beavers shot in the channel. Jack proudly explains how he'd trained Lid to track and how he'd found the evidence.

We tell her about the way the kits reacted to the sound of running water at home and how we set up the iPod experiment in their pool. And then we show her how we did the experiment in the river. We explain how Aaron figured out how to imitate the same sound out here.

"Okay, so you can . . . what? You direct the beavers where to build? You're saying you control them?"

"I just understand them," I say. "The point is not to control them, but to stop the beavers from damming in the wrong places where it wrecks people's property. Or when they flood roads. If we can stop them from making people angry, no one can say we need to get rid of them."

It's satisfying to share these thoughts with someone who listens.

Carrie taps her chin in thought. "Could you do it again?"

"I think so," I say.

"Well, let's find out."

We pile back into Carrie's truck and drive to the Township office to find the inspectors and road engineers — all two of them. The other secretary peers over her glasses with disapproval. Lid grins at her.

Next, we go back to the Birch Street culvert and explain it again to them. After that, things start to happen.

They take us to Catkin Street, where they've been fighting with beavers blocking that culvert all season. They have us repeat the experiment there. Setting it up this time is easier because they've got stake drivers that help pound the poles into the river. Aaron explains how he'd used the natural flow of water around the stakes to set up the sounds. They shake their heads, having a hard time believing how we know this stuff.

Later, when the inspectors see that once again the beavers made dams overnight and left the culvert alone, even more people get involved.

Pretty soon, we're standing in front of the whole town council explaining how we did it. Someone mentions it's a low-water year, so that might explain the beavers' actions. City plans and drawings are brought out and they argue among themselves about adding drain pipes, controlling water levels, and bottom lines, which Jack thinks is pretty funny until he realizes they're talking about budgets, not butts.

The next several days are a whirlwind. The Township makes plans to build a series of dams on top of drains. The drains are long tubes with plugs on the end that they can unscrew and open when needed. They direct the beavers where to build. Then, once the beavers make the dams, there's a way to control water levels and avoid flooding just by unplugging the drains. It's like releasing water out of a bathtub.

A few days later, my family and I get ready to watch the local evening news. It'd been such a crazy week, I barely had time to mourn the fact that I'd missed the whole Jane Goodall gala. Though every day I think about poor Xena. I want to make her short life mean something.

"It's on!" yells Marley.

Dad's crashing around searching for his phone to video the segment. He rushes into the den and we all settle down to watch.

I gape at the image on the screen. There we all are. Aaron, his orange hair crazy in the wind, his freckles being slowly devoured by the red creeping up his face. Jack, his gaze flighty and unfocused, picking at a scab on his meaty elbow. And me just looking weird in my ANIMALS ARE PEOPLE TOO T-shirt and my eyes the size of feed pans.

Lid's completely himself, not realizing he's on TV.

He starts retching, his whole body convulsing till he pukes up something slimy. Then he gives a wide, happy smile.

"What do you like about beavers?" The announcer holds the microphone in front of me.

"Beavers are amazing," I say nervously. "They talk a lot and they love their families."

Next to me, Jack and Aaron have frozen smiles as they stare at the camera.

"They're the only animals that can change the area where they live so much." Once I start talking about beavers, I appear to relax. "They can make ponds from a tiny stream, which is important because it makes a habitat for a ton of other animals to live. If there's no rain, they keep a place from drying up. All the animals depend on them! They're the world's best engineers. They're definitely not the smelliest!"

I cringe, watching myself on screen. "Is that how my voice sounds?"

"Every day," Dad says. He tweaks my nose.

I swat his hand, then focus back to the news.

"They have these fingers," TV-me continues. "They're

just like our hands. They can do so many things. And they're so smart—they can look at a problem and come up with three ways to solve that problem."

I see myself take a breath and get ready. "I know all this because I've been looking after beaver kits that were orphaned." I go on to relate the story about how Cooler helped me at the wire fence that day.

"You see, they're loyal to their family, and watch out for and protect each other. And they need *us* to protect *them*."

"Oh, honey, well done," Mom says.

I start to grin, then freeze when I hear the announcer.

"This twelve-year-old girl, the mastermind of the new project, is now on call as a consultant for the Township. They're calling her the Beaver Whisperer. She may have solved the town's problems and helped a whole community of beavers live in harmony with humans. Willow Grove News. Back to you, Jeff."

As I take in the reality of what just happened, I realize I've been training for this moment my whole life—this chance to talk for the animals and teach people about how we can help them.

I wish Nana were here to see it. Maybe I'll just email Jane Goodall and tell her about it all.

"Madison Lewis, *Beaver Whisperer.*" Dad pulls me in for a hug.

"Mastermind?" Marley snorts. "Master pain in my butt is more like it." But the shine in her eyes gives her away.

# 30

AFTER SEVERAL HOURS IN THE CAR, DAD and I are almost there.

He said he'd been wishing for a road trip since our Stratton plans were canceled.

Mom knew more than I thought about animal rehabbers. She didn't just hand Phrag and Cooler over to the Township, but arranged for them to go to a licensed wildlife rehabilitation facility called the Wilder Center.

I'm nearly jumping out of my seat in anticipation of seeing the kits again, and seeing the place where they're living. For the millionth time I peek inside the plastic tub to make sure the aquatic sedges we're bringing them are still fresh. Mr. Kang had dropped them off, along with a bone for "that hero dog."

He'd said that thanks to us kids getting the culprit charged, he had the restitution money to plant more trees. When he explained that he'd been the loudest opposition to the town council's plan for a beaver bounty, it all made sense.

Dan had been trying to change his mind. He wanted Mr. Kang to agree that beavers were a nuisance by making him think they'd ruined his landscaping. Good thing Mr. Kang was smarter than Dan. Though, I suspect most people are smarter than Dan.

As we pull off the highway and follow a long driveway, I see a large fenced field on one side and an enclosure with a pond on the other.

"There's Mr. Lee," Dad says, parking the car.

A short, balding man is there to greet us. "Hello, you must be Madison." He gives me a kind smile, then turns to Dad. "The rehabber community sadly misses your mother, Mr. Lewis."

"Thank you. So do we all," Dad says, squeezing my hand.

I feel a little unsure suddenly, wondering what Mr. Lee will think of me being just a kid. Until he says,

"The philosophy we try to promote here is responsible stewardship."

My heart leaps to hear him repeat something that Nana always said. Phrag and Cooler are in the right place.

"Exactly!" I say.

"If more people thought like you and did their part in their own backyards and communities to help wildlife, we'd be much better off. Of course," he adds, "we frown on people keeping wildlife. That usually does more harm to the animals than good. Though I suppose in this instance, with your background, it's a special circumstance." He opens the gate to the enclosure.

I scan over the secondary fencing surrounding the pond, searching for signs of the kits. His next words stop me.

"I'm hoping later on you can come educate my interns about your work with the Township."

I gasp. All this time I'd been on my own, wishing I had someone to learn from. And now here's a rehabber with interns, and he wants *me* to teach *them* what *I* know?

"Uh, sure," I squeak, not trusting my voice to say more.

"Great. They're looking forward to meeting the Beaver Whisperer." Mr. Lee meets my eyes and I see his understanding.

We continue toward the pond. In the center there's a beaver lodge replica built on a platform. My heart starts to pound.

"Your beavers seem to be enjoying their new habitat. They're always so busy. Ah, here they are now." Dr. Lee points to the far end of the enclosure.

Two familiar fur balls approach the water. Cooler spots me first. He dives in and swims toward my side of the pond, Phrag right behind him.

"Phrag! Cooler!" I race to greet them.

Crying, they waddle out of the water. *Meeeeee, meeeeee, meeee!* They stick their large noses through the fence toward me and I touch their faces. My heart squeezes. They look bigger. And happy.

Phrag grabs my hand with soft fingers.

"Look at you guys in your new home!" I say. "It's perfect!"

Satisfied with a quick pat, both beavers turn and dive back into the water. It's bittersweet to watch them disappear inside their lodge. I've wanted them to have the room to come and go as they wished, to live somewhere they could be beavers and not be locked secretly inside a tin shed. I want them to learn everything.

But I still miss them so much.

My throat feels tight as I imagine them growing up smart enough to one day return to live in the wild.

A week later my friends and I are sitting in the boat, fishing by the channel. The heavy sound of Lid's panting is getting hard to ignore.

He's sprawled on his side, ribs chugging. His head is wedged in the shade beneath Aaron's seat.

"Never catch anything with all that noise," Aaron complains.

"He's hot," Jack says.

"No wonder, with all that fur. Hey, let's shave him."

"Let's shave you." Jack reels his bobber in slowly.

Aaron frowns and pats his hair. "I'd sunburn."

"So would Lid."

"Not if we shave his bottom half. Like, just his underparts." Aaron's warming up to the idea.

"Then he'd be black and pink," I chime in.

Aaron rubs the fur on Lid's chest backwards to see the pink skin beneath. "Pink as a pig. That's embarrassing," Aaron murmurs.

My phone rings. I dig it out of my pack.

"Hello?" a worried voice says. "I was told to call this number. There's a baby deer hiding in the grass at the back of my yard. With no mom around. You think it's orphaned? Should I rescue it?"

"No! The main thing to do is leave it alone. The mom hid it there so she could go eat."

Jack gives me a side-eye.

"Probably," I amend. "Just keep tabs on it from a window till she comes back."

I hang up and Jack rolls his head back in feigned boredom. "That's the second call this week."

"Want to be my secretary?"

"There needs to be more poaching cases to solve. I have a special skill set that's not being utilized." Jack spits for emphasis, and then adds, "At least I'm still the best spitter."

"That would be Aaron," I remind him. Aaron grins.

"Challenge accepted." Jack sets down his rod. "Farthest loogie gets to drive the boat back."

The boat has drifted farther into the channel, and the beaver lodge that started it all comes into view.

"Aim toward the lodge," Jack says, over the sound of Aaron already making expert horking noises, bringing up something big.

We all face the water, Jack looking serious. Aaron holds his nasty prize on his tongue. A slapping tail draws my attention to three torpedo-shaped bodies on the surface cruising by.

"Look!" I say, contest forgotten. "Someone's taken advantage of an empty house and moved in."

At the sound of my voice, one of the beavers veers off and approaches. The larger beaver tries to put itself between us, but the small one keeps coming.

I hold my breath.

Aaron makes a swallowing motion.

The three of us watch as the beaver swims right up

to our boat. Even Lid sits up to study the little brown fuzz ball, his expressive eyebrows raised high.

The kit floats on the surface and peers at me. My heart leaps.

"Xena," I whisper. "Is that you?"

She hums. I recognize her now from the look on her face. In her way, she's saying hello and wants me to stop worrying about her. All this time, I thought these wild beavers had killed her. But it seems Xena got very lucky. They'd adopted her instead.

"Is this your new family? Thank you for telling me you're okay."

Xena turns and joins the other two beavers waiting for her. I watch them go until they dive near the lodge. I know what they're doing underwater. I know exactly what it feels like to swim up that tunnel into the dark little room. Xena is safe at home with her new family.

Jack, Aaron, and I give each other air high-fives.

Lid briefly thumps his tail on the bottom of the boat before he resumes his panting.

# AUTHOR'S NOTE

This story was inspired by a number of different sources.

I was intrigued after watching an episode of David Suzuki's *The Nature of Things*. It was about a real-life beaver whisperer who helped a town move from being in a war with beavers to living with them in harmony.

In 2001 while I was working as a conservation offi-cer in Kenora, Ontario, Canada, I met a real-life animal rehabilitator named Lil Anderson who wrote about her experiences with beaver kits. Her stories have stayed with me for years.

I appreciate Lil's time answering my questions while I researched and prepared to write this book. Parts of it were inspired from Lil's experiences, such as the bathtub scene, with a beaver plugging the drain with another beaver. Lil allowed me to borrow a phrase she coined in her first book: "uppy uppy arms." For further reading, I'd suggest both of her books, *Beavers Eh to Bea* and *Pond Memories*.

Thanks to the staff at the Science North Center in Sudbury, Ontario, for introducing me to their beavers and showing me their routine with the animal ambassadors in their care.

I'm also thankful for the time and assistance from Michele Grant, another animal rehabilitator with experience caring for a beaver kit named Timber. I especially want to mention that the scene with Cooler helping Madison over the fence was directly inspired by Michele's true experience with Timber. I felt it important to show the astounding intelligence of these remarkable animals.

My family lived on a lake where I grew up, slightly feral. I'd spend hours outside observing animals such as beavers. That is ultimately where Madi's story was born. The beavers on my lake were typically busy making dams across the channel into the next lake. This annoyed my dad to no end since he wanted to navigate through the channel. Forty years later, I'm still arguing with him about how cool beavers are.

# THE DOS OF WILDLIFE

**DO** make sure the baby is truly in need of rescuing. Animals like deer fawns and rabbits are most likely waiting for their mother to return. Animals like squirrels might just need to be reunited if they've fallen out of a nest. Keep pets away from the area and watch for up to twenty-four hours to see if a mom returns.

**DO** have an animal carrier or box ready before you attempt to help the baby. Have a towel on hand if you need to scoop them up. Wear gloves — safety first!

**DO** no harm. Avoid feeding or giving fluids. Things like cow's milk can cause diarrhea and further dehydrate the baby.

**DO** keep the carrier or box in a warm, quiet place. Wildlife are stressed around people and pets because they are seen as predators.

**DO** call a wildlife rehabilitator in your area. They have the expertise to help. If you can't contact a rehabber, find a wildlife center online and see if they have further instructions on the species you have found.

**DO** remember that many animals seem cute and cuddly, but they need to remain wild.

Reprinted with permission from the Wild for Life Rehabilitation Center, Rosseau, Ontario, Canada.

Another good source of information is the Michigan Department of Natural Resources (MI DNR) Keep Wildlife Wild program.

# Don't Miss More Great Adventure Novels by
# Terry Lynn Johnson

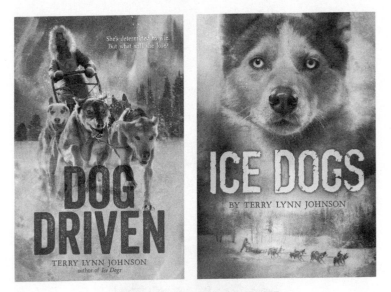

She's determined to win.
But what will she lose?

# DOG
# DRIVEN

## TERRY LYNN JOHNSON
author of *Ice Dogs*

# PRAISE FOR *DOG DRIVEN*

A Junior Library Guild Selection

★ "Suspenseful. . . . A fast-moving, thematically rich tale set at the intersection of ability and disability."

—*Kirkus Reviews,* starred review

★ "Readers will feel the cutting icy wind and the obstacles on the trail, and they'll hold their breath to see if McKenna stays safe. . . . Like Paulsen's *Winterdance,* Johnson shows the deep bonds and trust between musher and dogs, while also shedding light on a little-known genetic eye disorder. . . . [A] harrowing adventure."

—*Booklist,* starred review

"Captivating."

—*School Library Journal*

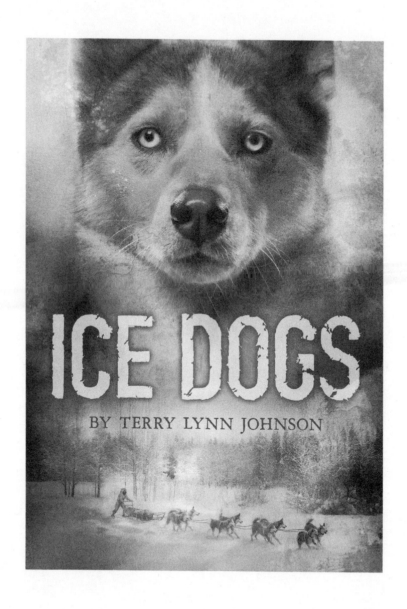

# ICE DOGS

## BY TERRY LYNN JOHNSON

# PRAISE FOR *ICE DOGS*

"A top-notch survival story."

—*Horn Book*

"Emotionally satisfying and insightful,

this story has staying power."

—*Booklist*

"A thoroughly engaging and incredibly suspenseful

survival story. . . . Johnson writes from a deep well of

experience. Well-crafted, moving, and gripping."

—*Kirkus Reviews*

# Sled Dog

# School

Will Matt's new
business make him the
leader of the pack?

## TERRY LYNN JOHNSON

Best-selling author of *Ice Dogs*

# PRAISE FOR *SLED DOG SCHOOL*

**A Junior Library Guild Selection**

"Themes of friendship and problem-solving are
slipped effortlessly into the funny and fresh plot,
and authentic off-the-grid details bring the story
to life. A tale of loyalty and friendship . . .
that hits all the right notes."

—*Kirkus Reviews*

# Go on an Adventure
## with Terry Lynn Johnson

# PRAISE FOR *SLED DOG SCHOOL*

**A Junior Library Guild Selection**

"Themes of friendship and problem-solving are
slipped effortlessly into the funny and fresh plot,
and authentic off-the-grid details bring the story
to life. A tale of loyalty and friendship . . .
that hits all the right notes."

**—*Kirkus Reviews***

# Go on an Adventure
## with Terry Lynn Johnson